MATCH POINT

RL BURGESS

Bella
BOOKS
2016

Bella Books, Inc.
P.O. Box 10543
Tallahassee, FL 32302

Printed in the United States of America on acid-free paper.

First Bella Books Edition 2016

Editor: Shelly Rafferty
Cover Designer: Linda Callaghan

ISBN: 978-1-59493-483-4

About the Author

At the age of 22, RL's friend shouted her to a visit with Rainbow Psychic. Rainbow held RL's hand across a worn Formica table and told her she would be a writer, describing the life she would have, sitting on her porch with a fat Labrador and a swing seat. A musician at the time, RL felt vaguely disappointed, shrugging off Rainbow's vision to pursue her dreams of touring the world in a band. Fourteen years later, her world touring accomplished, RL found herself pacing her house in the evenings while her beloved five year old son slept, wondering what to do with herself. Her partner suggested she write. And the rest is history.

NB: Whilst they do not yet have a Labrador or a swing seat, they all live happily in Melbourne, Australia with a perfectly functioning porch and two happy cats.

Dedication

For Grandma, who gave me my first romance novel.

Acknowledgements

Ultimate thanks go to my partner Sam, for teaching me about tennis, encouraging me to write and being an absolute rock of incredible support. Your heart truly is gold.

And to my editors, Shelly and Jackie, thanks for guiding me through the tough spots and showing me how to dig deeper.

Lastly, thank you to Bella Books, for saying yes!

PROLOGUE

Eight months earlier

Jodi pressed the phone to her ear with a shaky hand. Please be home, she thought as she listened to it ring, once, twice. Please be home.

"Hello?" The sound of her sister's voice filled Jodi with relief.

"Jodi? What's wrong?" Ally's voice was concerned. "What's happened?"

"Tara's left me." Jodi choked out. "It's over."

"Oh sis, I'm so sorry." Ally genuinely did sound sorry. "I'll be there as soon as I can. Two hours, tops."

"Can you bring the van?" Jodi asked, "I've got some stuff."

"Of course!"

Ally was there in an hour and a half, having battled the I-80 traffic from Sacramento to San Francisco with Goliath-like determination. She ran up the stairs to give her sister a long tight hug.

Together they loaded Jodi's bags into the back of the van and Jodi had left a note for Tara on the kitchen bench: *You keep the rest. Jodi.*

Jodi stayed with Ally and her husband for a few weeks, holed up in the spare room in their spacious home in Sacramento. She was comforted by the old feeling of being tucked under her big sister's wing, hiding out from the world as she licked her wounds. Jodi couldn't face house hunting and decided she wouldn't look for a new place until she was ready to buy. She decided instead to find a hotel and set herself up somewhere totally new, somewhere that held no memories of Tara.

Thankfully, Sacramento had a wealth of comfortable, nondescript hotels to choose from. Jodi picked a place that looked architecturally interesting on the outside, while still subscribing to the classic hotel formula of white walls and beige bedspreads. The hotel was right in the city center, a place where she had spent little time since her teen years. She and Ally had grown up on the outskirts of Sacramento, but in her twenties she had always preferred the allure of San Francisco's night life when she got a rare night off from her grueling tennis schedule. And now, it felt somehow easier to be staying in a hotel, like she was just visiting, as if the reason she was lost and confused was because she was a tourist, not because she was suffering from a broken heart.

Settling into her temporary new home, Jodi allowed herself to drift, freewheeling through the pain and the shock, wandering through the fog inside her as she tried to remember who she was. She couldn't quite touch it. She had spent so many years denying herself, pushing away what she really wanted in order to fit in with Tara.

One morning as Jodi sat on the floor by the window, pressing her head against the glass, she watched the people pass by on the street below. She felt aimless and indecisive, not really knowing what to do with herself. For the last five years her free time had been filled with Tara, with doing the things that Tara wanted to do. Watching a man with a tennis racket step out onto the curb and into a waiting taxi, she suddenly realized she was free to choose to be or do anything she wanted. She could be like any of those people. More to the point, she could be herself. Deep down, a little piece of her abruptly buzzed with excitement.

Jason, she thought. I need to call Jason.

With trembling fingers, Jodi punched in the numbers she still knew by-heart, hoping Jason hadn't changed his number, hoping he'd be receptive to her call. When she had left the game five years earlier, she had left abruptly. Jason could be forgiven for being angry with her: he had been an amazingly supportive coach and had been patiently persistent with her when she had started to withdraw, yet she had turned her back on him and left him in the dark. He hadn't deserved that. He had been much more than just her coach. He had been her friend.

Things had gotten tough back then. She had been at the top of her game but injuries had been plaguing her, petty strains and tears causing havoc with her body and mindset, leaving her irritable, unconfident, and unfocused.

Jason had tried to help her, gently steering her in the right direction and counseling her to stay calm, but Jodi felt she was slipping and the feeling made her crazy. She pushed herself to practice harder and longer, exacerbating her injuries and ultimately undermining her game.

Jason had protested and tried to intervene. "Jodi," he began. His frustration had been clear. "You're an amazing tennis player. But you need to cut yourself some slack or you're going to run yourself into the ground."

Jodi hadn't listened to him.

And then Tara. Tara with all the right curves in all the right places. Tara with her distractingly long, honey-colored locks and piercing green eyes. Tara with the perfectly tanned skin and neverending legs that seemed designed to be wrapped around Jodi. Tara who wanted to comfort Jodi and who had effortlessly extracted her from the game Jodi had found herself at war with, plucking her from the struggle as if she were a child to be picked up and tucked under her arm.

Jodi and Tara had met at a house party in the hills of Berkeley, where Jodi knew only a few people and felt out of her depth. She had won her match that day by the skin of her teeth and felt uneasy and awkward at the party. Admiring the view through the huge open French windows, Jodi had responded to the magic by sneaking off to a dark corner of the deck to enjoy the sparkle of San Francisco's lights against the blackness of the Pacific Ocean. Out of the darkness, she had heard a sigh next to her.

"Oh, I'm sorry," Jodi had said, startled. "I didn't realize there was anybody else here."

"That's okay." A woman stepped out of the shadows. "I'm just enjoying this incredible view."

Jodi had stared at the woman, her pupils captivated by her sudden appearance. The darkness of the night smoothed off lines and softened edges and Jodi felt she was looking at possibly the most beautiful woman she had ever met.

"I'm Jodi." She offered her hand to shake.

"Tara." The woman took Jodi's hand in both of hers and held it. "I know who you are. You're the tennis player." Tara turned Jodi's hand over in hers, tracing the rough calluses that ran across the palm of Jodi's hand with her thumbs.

"From my racket," Jodi stammered, suddenly nervous.

"It's too noisy around here for me tonight," Tara said, still rubbing her thumbs across Jodi's palm.

Jodi tried to suppress a shiver.

"Are you cold?" Tara asked.

"No, I… you…" Jodi felt slightly out of her body.

Turning her hand over, Tara linked her fingers through Jodi's and pulled her closer. "It's noisy here," she said again. "Would you like to go and get a drink somewhere quieter? I know a pretty little place right on the bay."

And they left, just like that.

Jodi hadn't been an unwilling participant. Tara had gradually pulled her away from tennis, and Jodi let herself be pulled, as if their hands were still intertwined at the party. In the end, Jodi's state of turmoil made it quite easy for her to let go of tennis. And Tara had been subtle but determined to have Jodi all to herself.

Before long, Jodi found herself living in Tara's luxury townhouse overlooking the bay. Tara's taste for the finer things in life was evident in all that adorned the space, from the Wedgwood crystal glassware they filled with champagne and clinked together in the evenings, to the modern contemporary art that lined the crisp white walls. A highly successful and driven real-estate agent, Tara worked long hours, moonlighting with clients and scouting for high-finance opportunities. She didn't have time to travel with Jodi to out-of-town tournaments, which were too long and too far away. Jodi's practice interfered in their weekend plans: boating with prospective clients or entertaining other industry big-wigs. Jodi's strict athlete's diet and eating regimes were awkward for dinners out and socializing, and most of all, it was hard to make love when her body was aching and exhausted from grueling four-hour matches and week-long tournaments.

It had just seemed easier to focus on Tara and the life they were planning together than to fight her demons on the tennis court. Jodi made ridiculous last-minute excuses to Jason for pulling out of matches; she became unreliable and her ranking plummeted. Finally, she stopped returning his calls and allowed herself to fade out of his life.

She knew she had hurt him. They had been through so much together, training hard at all hours of the day, working on her game through the depths of searing pain to the soaring heights of glorious successes that were as much his as hers. Jason had invested in her, believed in her, and made her his number one player. Yet she had left him wondering what the hell was going on, without so much as a thank you or a goodbye. Jodi had never told him she was gay. Never told him about Tara. Never told him she was suffering. She just stopped turning up.

And now, as she sat on the floor of her hotel room, listening to the phone ring on the other end, she wondered if he would ever accept her apology, if her explanations would be too little, too late. It has been far too long and Jodi was ashamed and embarrassed.

She was just about to hang up when a voice on the other end breathlessly answered "Hello?"

"Jase," she stumbled, not sure how to go on. "Uh, it's me. Jodi."

CHAPTER ONE

Jodi felt a trickle of warm sweat run slowly down between her shoulder blades. The weather gods had said today was going to be a scorcher, and they weren't wrong. The heat swam up off the court in waves, burning through the soles of her shoes and baking her feet. She licked her parched lips and squinted her eyes against the harsh sun, focusing all of her energy across the court on her opponent, Kerry Jefferson, who was preparing her stance for service. C'mon, Jodi thought, let's do this, Jefferson.

Jodi danced gently from side to side on the balls of her feet, feeling a tiny breath of hot wind lift the edge of her shirt. She watched and waited, poised to leap in to action. The ball flew wildly towards her and over the baseline.

"Out!" the umpire called.

Her opponent grimaced in frustration. Jodi felt a flicker of commiseration. So close, she thought. We're almost there. She released the breath she didn't realize she had been holding and checked her grip on the racket. The heat was making Jodi's hands slippery and she wiped them on her shorts. Her muscles were tired and crying out for this game to be over. *One more point and this match is mine.* Just hold on, hold on, she told herself.

Hearing the thump of the ball on Kerry's racket, Jodi threw her body across the court, stretching her arm out wide and whipping the ball back across the net with huge force. Kerry lunged for it and scooped it up high, sending Jodi to the back of the court to catch the bounce and smash it back over the net.

"Game! Set! Match: Richards!" the umpire cried.

Relief flooded through Jodi and she dropped her racket, victoriously shaking her fist in the air. She looked up into the crowds and waved, feeling a surge of elation course through her. Catching the eye of Jason, her coach and her long-time friend, she pumped her fist again and blew him a kiss. He gave her the thumbs up. Walking to the net to shake hands with Kerry, Jodi realized she was utterly exhausted.

"Great match," Jodi said, hugging her friend over the net. "It was a close one."

"Thanks," Kerry mumbled, returning the hug, clearly disappointed and tired. "You did great."

They'd known each other on the tennis circuit for many years and Jodi could see the frustration and pain etched across Kerry's face. She didn't want to think about the number of times she had looked like that in the past.

"You might need to give yourself some more time to heal that ankle." Jodi gave her friend a sympathetic squeeze before they both headed off the court to grab their bags and greet their fans.

The match had been a long one and Jodi could feel a wobble in her legs as she sat on her bench for a moment, putting her rackets back into their cases and draping a towel around her neck. *Thanks Nan,* she thought, taking a moment to send up her ritualistic, post-match gratitude to the woman she felt was always watching over her. *We did it.* She gulped down some water and rubbed her face with the towel, then looked up into the crowds again with a rush of joy as she noted the banners, the people still clapping and calling out her name. She had missed this. She waved at them again and grinned, holding up her towel like a trophy. Slinging her racket bag across her shoulder, Jodi stood up and gave the crowd one last wave. Heading off the court, she stopped to sign tennis balls and shake hands with the people she passed in the corridor on the way.

At the locker rooms, Jason picked Jodi up and spun her around. "Jodi! You little champ!" he said.

"Whoa," Jodi replied with a laugh as her rackets banged against the locker room wall. "Easy, tiger!"

Jason slapped her on the shoulder and handed her an energy bar.

"Great match!" he enthused. "You smashed it out of the park today, Jodes. I was a bit worried about you at the end of the first set when you double-faulted, but you pulled it back like a pro and cleaned up. It was 105 degrees on court today. Did you feel it?" His blue eyes sparkled with excitement and Jodi had a sudden picture of what he must have looked like as a little boy. His sandy hair flopped endearingly across his forehead, just shading the top of his eyebrows, a bristly five o'clock shadow somewhat at odds with his youthful face. "You looked amazingly cool," he said.

Jodi shook her head, swallowing her mouthful. "I felt the heat but I didn't, if you know what I mean?" She sat down on the bench, pulling off her shoes as she spoke. "I knew I was sweating and my feet were hot but I just went with it, you know? Actually I sort of liked it that hot. I felt like I could really feel my whole body," she trailed off. "I think I'm a bit dehydrated though, I need more fluids."

Jason dug into his bag and pulled out a cold bottle of coconut-flavored sports drink. "Here you go."

"Ooh, my favorite, thanks." Jodi took the bottle gratefully, twisting it open and tipping her head back to let the cool sweet liquid run down her throat. She sighed, leaning against Jason a little. "Can we go home now?" she asked.

"Sure," he said, "as soon as you've dealt with the thirty reporters, ten tennis officials and five hundred fans waiting for you outside this door, you can go home straightaway!" Jason chuckled. "You don't make it in to the finals of a tournament like this, after five years off the courts, and get to slink away like the loser, Jodes. Especially to an at home crowd!"

"I'll go get decent." She cracked him a lopsided smile and ambled towards the shower.

Jodi was tired, but she was excited. Jase was right, she thought, as she turned the shower taps on hard, reveling under the strong stream of cool water. She shook out her braid, working shampoo through the length of her long dark hair, enjoying the ache of tiredness in her arms. Today had been a huge occasion and she was glad people had shown up to support her and were waiting to talk to her, to celebrate with her after the match. It was her chance to show she was still finals' material and thankfully, she had nailed it. A small thrill fluttered through her. I won! she thought. The months of training and preparation had paid off and the ball was rolling.

Entering the tournament just last week, Jodi had not been immune to the murmurs of surprise and questioning looks. After five years off the court, no one had expected her to come back, let alone come back as a winner. She almost didn't really expect it herself. And yet, here she was, four wins into her first US Open wild card qualifying tournament, lining up for the finals in two days' time. Jodi didn't dare think about what would come next, strangely superstitious about jinxing her future by imagining it too vividly. If I picture it in my mind, it might not happen, she thought. She knew she was at odds with the current self-help trend of positive thinking, but it was a quirky little habit she had picked up as a child and found she couldn't shake.

She had first discovered this "power" when she was waiting for letters from her father, after they had gone to live with Nan. Jodi had no recollection of her mother becoming sick. At four years old, she had been too young to really understand what was happening when the cancer had set in. Her father had been so grief-stricken by their mother's illness that he sent Jodi and Ally to Nan's, unable to look after both his daughters and his increasingly ill wife.

After her mom's death, her father had seemed to fade away. Burying himself in work, he took on more travel assignments, leaving the girls for longer and longer with Nan until it had made sense for them to move in permanently.

Nan had been everything to both girls: grandmother, mother, and father, too, really. She had done her best to fill all the holes in their lives while everything had fallen down around them. She had sung the girls to sleep, driven them to school, helped with their homework, baked and cooked and cleaned, and sewn without a word of complaint; even though this was, Jodi realized much later, the second time she was raising children. Looking back, Jodi realized that Nan had always put their grief before her own, their needs at the forefront of everything, even when she must have been aching with the loss of her own daughter.

Jodi and Ally's father had occasionally sent postcards and even small letters from the various exotic places he visited for conferences and workshops, and Jodi would wait for them anxiously. Walking up the hill from school in the afternoons, she would tell herself not to imagine the letterbox with a letter in it, just to clear her mind and let it be, annoying herself when a picture of a postcard would suddenly appear, unbidden in her mind. She found that the days when she hadn't been thinking of her father at all were usually the ones when a letter would appear. Jodi had hung on to this strange theory ever since.

One step at a time, she told herself as she turned off the taps and wrapped herself in a towel. Just focus on each moment as it comes. She had felt guilty when she had abandoned her tennis career to be with Tara, like she had been somehow disloyal to Nan, and all the time and effort she had put in over the years to support Jodi in her burgeoning tennis career. "If you want this my girl, then let's go get it," Nan used to say, as they had all packed up the car to drive to an out-of-town tournament. Jodi couldn't quite think about Nan when she lived with Tara. The memories had been too painful and she had felt like the life she was living was somehow at odds with the values Nan had raised her with. Nan would have wanted to know what her plans were, what she wanted to do with her life now that she was done with tennis, but Jodi had shut out those thoughts and allowed herself to be steered along by Tara.

But now, with her first comeback match behind her, she let herself imagine that soft, increasingly wrinkled face she had loved so much.

"I'm back, Nan," she whispered as she stopped for a moment in front of the mirror. She studied her face for the old signs of likeness. She knew they had shared the long straight nose so characteristic of her mother's family line, and of course, there were the dark brown eyes. Even when she had been close to the end of her life, Nan's eyes had still held their vivid shine.

Drying herself and pulling on clean shorts and a fresh t-shirt, Jodi focused her thoughts, trying to prepare herself for the press conference to come. She knew they were going to ask her some difficult questions, and she'd been over them again and again. *Do you think you can do it after all this time away? Why did you leave? Why did you come back?* She knew they wouldn't hesitate to get straight to the point. For a moment, Jodi flashed back to Tara's face, feeling the familiar stab of pain in her heart as she replayed their final conversation.

"You're just never really there," Tara said flatly, defending her actions when Jodi had discovered the affair.

"But what do you mean?" Jodi asked, crying in confusion and frustration. *"I'm always here. All I am is here. Day in, day out, I'm here; doing things for us, keeping our lives perfect."*

"Yes, you're here," Tara said wearily, as if it were an effort just to speak the words. *"You're here, but your mind is always somewhere else. Your heart is never really fully open. I'm sorry Jodi, but I've fallen in love with her and I can't do this anymore. We're done."*

And with that Tara walked coldly out the door, carefully closing it behind her, as deliberately as she had closed Jodi out of her life. Jodi was devastated, her heart was smashed, but there was a part of her that knew Tara was right. A part of Jodi was numb, and felt like it had been for years.

Jodi shook her head and took a deep breath, letting go of the memory. She reminded herself that she was prepared for this; she was ready to face the questions about her long absence and now, her return. Fixing herself with a steely gaze in the mirror, she ran a brush through her long, straight brown hair, twisting it up into a bun. You can do this, she told herself, and headed out to meet the waiting group.

Jodi slid onto the plastic chair next to her coach, behind the table set up with microphones for the press conference.

"You ready?" Jason gave her arm a squeeze.

Her face was set with determination. "Bring it on."

"Okay, ladies and gentleman," Jason spoke into the microphone, bringing the waiting press group to attention, "Jodi has ten minutes to answer your questions today and then I'm sure you'll appreciate she needs to get her rest and focus for the final match on Saturday. So who's first?"

A bunch of hands shot up.

Jason chose a young reporter at the front for the first question. "Yes, Patrick. Fire away." Jason knew all the reporters' names, having been in the business for a long time.

"Um, Jodi," Patrick called, "what made you decide to come back to tennis?"

Jodi looked out at the crowd of reporters, taking in the flashing cameras and microphones pointed her way. Dipping her head, she spoke slowly in to the microphone. "I thought I could still win."

The crowd laughed and the questions continued to come thick and fast, with Jason picking people out of the group and handling the process smoothly. The media, she knew, had an insatiable desire for detail, and things could be misconstrued incredibly easily—so she approached every question with consideration and care as she gave her answers. They asked her to analyze her wins, her past losses, changes to her playing style, changes to her support team, and finally, after what had seemed like an hour, Jason called wrap-up.

"One last question folks." He scanned the crowd for someone who hadn't had a chance to speak yet. He singled out an older man with his hand up. "Oh yes, John, what have you got for us?"

"Right, thanks. Jodi," he asked, "why did you actually leave tennis?"

"Uh, well, I…" Jodi cleared her throat, and took a sip of water. "I left for love."

A murmur passed through the crowd and they waited expectantly for more, but she wasn't going to give it to them if she didn't have to.

"Er, and?" John pushed, digging for more.

She looked at her glass of water, noticing condensation droplets forming on the outside of the cool glass in the heat. She ran a finger down the outside of the glass and picked it up She took a small sip. "And that didn't work out. So I'm back," she stoically replied.

"And that's enough for today. Thanks, ladies and gents." Jason stood up, signaling the end to the conference. Together Jodi and Jason stood for a moment for the cameras. Jodi smiled and thanked them all for coming and for continuing to support her career. With a final wave, they left the building, hurrying into the cool air-conditioned car waiting for them outside the tennis center.

"That was great." Jason slid into the seat across from her as the car pulled away from the curb. "You said enough, you didn't say too much. Got to keep them guessing a bit, don't we?"

"Sure," Jodi replied, watching the people mill about the entrance to the building as they drove slowly past. She was beginning to feel numb with exhaustion, her win today an almost distant memory.

"Jodi! Jodi!" People pressed towards the car. "Sign my shirt!"

"Will you sign my ball?"

"Hey Jodi!"

"Stop the car please," Jodi called out to the driver, buzzing down her window. She reached through the opening and shook hands, signed shirts and balls and even a man's back with her permanent marker, smiling patiently as she thanked her fans and told them she had to get home for some pre-finals rest.

As the car slowly moved forward again, Jodi's head felt heavy. She wanted to lie down right there on the back seat, press her face into the leather, and sleep. She remembered those times when she was a kid, driving home late at night with Nan. She would undo her seatbelt and stretch out, her head touching one door and her feet touching the other as she drifted off to the quiet rumble of the tires on the road and the muted sounds of Nan and Ally talking in the front. They'd never let kids do that these days, Jodi thought.

She needed to get home now and relax, get away from the buzz and the hype and have some time to herself. Home, she thought ruefully to herself. Well, at least to her hotel room. Could you call a hotel room home? She had been there since leaving Ally's almost eight months before, which made it a kind of home, she guessed.

Jodi shuddered, remembering the night she had left the home she shared with Tara and gone to Ally's, how she had feverishly packed her clothes into bags, and shoved papers and books into boxes and shopping bags before she had rung Ally to pick her up.

"You alright?" Jason stretched his legs out in front of him as far as they could reach in the back of the luxury car.

As they sped silently through the streets of Sacramento towards her hotel, Jodi was filled with gratitude towards him. Not only had he listened to her when she had finally gotten up the courage to ring him, but he had accepted her apology. She had told him everything and he was gracious, if a little gruff.

"I don't make judgments about how you want to live your life, Jodi," he said when she had told him she was gay. "I just care how you play tennis. You could have told me, you know," his voice cracked.

"I know that now…" she said.

"Five years Jodi! It's been five years."

"Will you have me back?" she had asked in a small voice, daring to hope he would give her the answer she wanted.

"I never let you go." Jodi could hear the smile in his voice.

"Jodes?" His brow was a line of concern.

"Sorry. Daydreaming. I'm fine." She rubbed her hands across her eyes, "Just exhausted."

"I'm not surprised. It's been a huge day. In fact, it's been a huge week. And now we need to get you some R and R in time for Saturday's match. What are you doing for dinner tonight?"

"I think I'll just eat some leftovers and curl up on the couch with a movie. What I really need is a long hot bath and about fifty liters of fluids! I'd almost forgotten how intense it is to play in this heat!"

"Tomorrow we'll get the physio up in the morning to check you over and rub out the kinks before we hit the practice courts, okay?" Jason pushed his hair out of his eyes as he reached over to grab his tournament folder. "Kitchfield and Drummond are playing the semi-finals tomorrow at... um..." Jason scanned the folder, trailing his finger down the match lists until he hit upon the line he wanted. "11am, court five. I think we should be there. You'll be up against the winner for finals, so it's a good chance for us to study the play. How about we meet down at the practice court at 8am to hit some balls beforehand?"

"So, physio at 7am?" Jodi longed for a sleep-in but dismissed the feeling out of hand. She'd had five years of luxurious sleep-ins and what had that achieved? Nothing. All she had done was lie restlessly in bed, waiting for Tara to want to get up and start the day. Eventually she started sneaking out of bed early, while Tara still slept, careful to avoid the hand that would grab her and pull her back to bed for interminable snuggles if she accidentally woke her. Used to years of early morning tennis starts and hugely energetic days, it was a novelty at first, lying around in bed late into the mornings on the weekends, but it had quickly worn off, leaving her fidgety and uneasy in their king-sized bed.

"Why don't we ask the physio to come up straight after your shower so you're nice and supple? Do you want to have breakfast first? She could come at 6.30am to give you a full work-over before we hit," Jason said.

"Sounds good." Jodi felt a rush of gratitude towards him. It was good to be a team again. "Tomorrow I want to focus on service. I'm just not getting my feet right. I feel like I'm all set up and then suddenly I realize, half way through the toss, that I'm not in the right position and I'm off kilter. I think that's why I doubled faulted today," Jodi said.

"Let's do that then," Jason replied, noting it down in his folder.

The car neared Jodi's hotel and she looked forward to sinking into the hot tub, letting the heat and the bubbles do their magic on her shaky muscles.

"How's Sally coping in this heat?" At five months pregnant, Jason's petite wife was already quite big.

"She's definitely feeling it. She said to me this morning she can't decide which would be worse, being pregnant in this heat, or being married to someone who is pregnant in this heat!"

Jodi laughed. "Lucky you've got AC."

"Yes, and lucky I make such a good slave. Hey, I'd like to bring Miranda Ciccone to practice tomorrow. I'm thinking of moving her up to assistant coach and I want to see how she goes with planning out our practice schedule between now and Saturday. Is that cool with you? I mean, obviously I'll oversee her." Jason looked up from the folder he had been studying, seeking Jodi's approval. "I've had her analyzing your play for a while now, and she knows your style. I want to see if she can properly gauge your strengths and weaknesses and come up with a plan of attack."

"Miranda?" Jodi looked at Jason blankly, momentarily confused. Her eyebrows pulled together as she tried to place the name.

"You know, the chick who's been running my junior coaching team. You met her a couple of months ago when she was doing that early warm-up session with some of the juniors on the court next to ours."

"Oh yeah, her? You want to move her up? Who do you have to replace her?"

"I don't need to replace her at the moment, the juniors are tracking really well and we've got enough staff on the team to carry it while I try her out."

The car began to slow and pulled to the curb as Jodi gazed out of the window at her hotel, feeling strangely comforted by its familiar entrance arch and cobbled pavement.

"Sure, whatever you think will work." Jodi wasn't too bothered by who was installed as assistant coach as long as

Jason was in charge and they did what he said. She trusted his judgment. Gathering up her racket bags, Jodi slung her gym bag across her shoulders. "See you in the morning, coach man. Get some good sleep!" she said.

"You too, champ. You deserve it."

Jodi thanked the driver who held the door open for her as she slid out of the car. "Goodnight Sid," she called to him. "See you in the morning."

"Good night, Jodi" he replied, nodding to her as she headed into the hotel. "It's great to have you back."

Alone in the elevator Jodi punched in the twelfth floor and enjoyed the sensation of her stomach dropping as it shot upwards. She leaned her head against the cool mirrored glass and looked into her own eyes, searching through the earthy brown color for something within. She saw tiredness, but she also saw elation, and something else. Relief. She still had the knack; she could still pull the power serves, the smashes at the net and her trademark backhand, unofficially dubbed "the Richards slice." Miraculously, five years away from the court hadn't left her too old or too unfit, too staid to play the game. She still had her edge. Her fitness would come up, and she needed to keep working on her game, but she was holding her own and she was so damn relieved.

As she swiped herself into her suite, her cell phone buzzed from deep within her gym bag. She dug through the bag, spilling the contents out onto the floor.

"Ally!" she answered, seeing her sister's name on the screen.

"Sis! Congratulations." Ally's voice cheered down the line. "I wanted to stick around after the match but I knew you'd take ages talking to all those people. How are you? How are you feeling?"

"Starving." Jodi bundled up her gym bag and moved through the entrance hall, dumping it on the couch in the living room as she headed for the kitchen. "Starving, but awesome," she added.

"I'm so proud of you! I still can't believe you're doing this. God it's great to see you out there again."

"Aw, thanks sis. Thanks for being there today, it was super cool knowing you were in the crowd."

"Oh, I wouldn't have missed it! So what happens now? I'm confused. You've got the finals for this tournament and then what? How are we getting into the US Open again? Please tell me I don't need to buy tickets!"

Jodi laughed and opened the fridge, pulling out last night's quinoa and tofu salad from Wholefoods. She perched on the counter to eat and chat. "So you know I need to play this tournament, and then there are two others that I'll have to win," she said. "Those will give me the qualifying points I need to get the wild card entry into the Open... if I win them, that's is. Basically I've just got to put my head down and keep playing all the other tournaments in between—get my points and my skills up as high as I can."

"You'll win," her sister said confidently. "You have to win. I didn't buy tickets to the Open this year on purpose. I'm counting on you to get me in!"

"Well, okay then," Jodi laughed. "I guess I have no choice. I wouldn't want to deprive my only sister of her yearly New York holiday at the US Open."

"Exactly. So do whatever mumbo jumbo you have to do to get your butt over the line and let's go to New York, baby!"

"Got it," Jodi managed, smiling through a mouthful of food.

"Alright, I gotta go. Marty's taking me to dinner at the new steakhouse on the bay for our anniversary tonight. I know your little pescetarian heart is appalled by that, but you know me, I love a good juicy steak!"

"Lovely," Jodi replied sarcastically. "Thanks for reminding me."

"Anyway," Ally breezed, "now I need to squeeze myself into the kind of outfit I probably shouldn't be wearing at my age, but that hopefully says 'I know we've been married for fifteen years but with any luck you still find me the sexiest woman in the room,' and that's gonna take some work." Ally took a deep breath.

"Oh, as if he doesn't think that already. Marty's crazy about you. He has been since the moment you crashed your delivery van into his back fence."

"True! Okay, I think you're ace. See you Saturday."

"And I think you're fab," Jodi said, finishing their ritual. She put her phone down and slid off the bench. It was time for the hot tub.

CHAPTER TWO

Miranda swept her gaze across the line of young hopefuls in front of her. This group was her favorite. The cream of the crop. Her baby pro-tennis players. Her eyes settled on one particularly lanky youth who appeared to be pretty much all arms and legs. Like a spider, Miranda thought with amusement, but a spider who was playing excellent tennis these days. His arms could reach out to connect with the ball with an almost elastic stretch and his legs carried him across the court in graceful bounds. Or perhaps a colt, Miranda thought, not a spider.

"Ok guys. You've all worked really hard this week and I think we can all agree we're seeing some real progress. Becca, your serve is really sharpening up. I love the way you're dancing around the baseline and covering the whole court. Nick, excellent smash work today, and you're really nailing that powerhouse forehand. Jessie, killer on the backhand. I think next week we'll start to really focus on your footwork. Sarah and Nathan, those were some great rallies today, you really made each other work." Her eyes travelled the group once more and her gaze came back to the elastic boy. "And Thomas, you're player of the week," she announced.

Thomas' face lit up in a handsome young grin.

"You've shown consistent improvement and you're obvious-ly putting in the hard yards. It's really showing in your game." Miranda clapped Thomas on the shoulder and laughed as he blushed.

"Excellent! Thanks Coach," he said.

"You've earned it. You're all doing brilliantly, and I'd say if you keep up this pace, you're all on track for some big wins in the September Junior tournament rounds. So go hit the showers and get some dinner. Have a great weekend and I'll see you Monday."

"Thanks, coach," they chorused, turning to head for the clubhouse in a straggly, teenage bunch.

"Ooh and wait, before I forget, Jodi Richards won the semi-final today which means she's playing the final on Saturday. You should all come down! If anyone needs a ticket, pop in to see me before you leave tonight and I'll get you an entry pass from the office." She waved them off with a smile. "Now go get clean."

"You want some help picking up the balls, coach?" Jessie flicked a stray tennis ball up into the air with her racket and caught it deftly.

"I think I can get them today, Jessie. You go grab a shower before the hot water runs out! Great work today."

"Cool, well thanks again, coach." She tossed her ball into the ball bag and jogged backwards towards the clubhouse. "It was a really fun day. I'll come and grab one of those passes from you," she called.

"Great Jessie. It's important to support our own!"

Miranda strolled around the court, scooping up balls with her racket and hitting them lightly into the ball bag. She enjoyed this after-practice ritual. Usually she had the team help her tidy up the court so it would be done quickly, but this evening she was in no hurry and didn't mind a little alone time.

"Hey, Miranda!" her boss's voice called out from the steps of the clubhouse.

"Jase," she said, as she flicked her racket in a wave. "Congrats on today! Jodi must be stoked."

"She is. Hey listen, when you're done there can you come in and see me in the office?" Jason shaded his eyes from the setting sun as he looked across the court at her.

"Sure coach, I won't be long. Give me five minutes to grab the rest of these balls and I'll come up."

Jason disappeared back into the clubhouse. Just yesterday they'd spent an hour together, going over the junior team, tracking their progression, dividing up the coaching team and finalizing the game plan for September's tournament preparation. She couldn't imagine what he would want to see her again so soon. Probably something we missed, she thought and shrugged, jogging over to the back fence line to scoop up the remaining balls.

Hefting the big bag up onto the ball trolley, Miranda pushed it down to the equipment shed at the back of the court. She deposited the balls and locked it up for the night. She was excited. Her team was really shaping up and she knew there was some real talent in those teenage bodies. Some of them reminded of her of herself when she was sixteen: bursting out of her skin with energy, promise and passion for the game, keen to practice all day and talk tennis all night, staying up late to watch the international tournaments so she could study the moves of the pros and glean their tricks. She had been a fixture at her local club, heading straight from school to the courts each day to practice, working hard to qualify for the junior's pro team and her first big Junior Tournament match. She had even won a training scholarship from her club—a welcome relief for Miranda, whose parents were keen to support her but had been talking about her getting an after-school job to finance the ongoing club fees.

Each year she saved her pocket money for a weekend pass to the San Francisco City Open. She would catch the bus into San Francisco with her dad, where they would make a special father-daughter bonding weekend of it by staying with her dad's sister, Aunt Louise. Each day they would arrive at the tennis center early to get the best seats, and stay to watch back-to- back matches until, hungry and tired, they would make their way back to give the ever patient Aunt Louise a blow-by-blow account of the day over Chinese take-out. Miranda still remembered those weekends fondly.

Miranda's passion for the sport had never left her. At the age of twenty-nine, she still stayed up late watching tennis across the globe, but her prospects of becoming a major league tennis player herself had promptly been erased when she was diagnosed with non-Hodgkin lymphoma (NHL) just after her seventeenth birthday.

Suddenly she had been caught up in a whirlwind of doctors' visits, scans, tests and hospital stays, and eventually surgery, followed by months of intermittent chemotherapy treatment. It was harsh and frightening and she had felt sick for months on end, but Miranda had tried hard to be brave and stay positive. She remembered the feeling of despair as she woke up to find a handful of her own blonde hairs on the pillow, and the realization that she would no longer be a normal teenager. Her mom had come back from the store that same day with a shopping bag bulging with materials, dragged out the sewing machine and proceeded to sew up a bunch of bandanas from the patterns Miranda chose from the pile. They had all had fits of laughter when her dad had tried them on later that night, dancing around the house with his air guitar, pretending to be Axl Rose.

A long and frustrating road led back to recovery and full health. She had missed half a year of school and had to work hard to catch up and graduate with her friends. And she'd missed the boat on tennis. Yes, that ship had well and truly sailed. But she had still wanted to stay involved, so as her health returned she eventually joined a local club for the occasional friendly weekend match.

In Miranda's early twenties, her best friend Enid had convinced her to come with her as a tennis coach on a summer camp run by the local club, and she found that she loved teaching and working with the younger kids. From there she applied for a permanent coaching position at the club and was ecstatic to be accepted. She stayed on at the club, learning the ropes, becoming a competent, sought-after coach, and the kids loved her.

Three years ago, Enid had rung her in a tizz. "Meet me at Cafe Trioli after work," Enid demanded.

"I can't tonight. I promised the kids that tomorrow I would show them that video I made ages ago of the best finals moments over the last ten years, and I've got to go to mom and dad's and dig out the tape. Actually," she paused, suddenly struck by a thought, "I don't even know if the clubhouse has a video player! I really should upload that video to YouTube tonight."

"Miranda. Enough! Listen up, my friend. You need to meet me tonight, and I won't take no for an answer. I'll see you there at six sharp."

Miranda shook her head in bemusement. Enid was a firecracker, always full of wild ideas and schemes, not to mention her penchant for dramatic love affairs. She had no idea what Enid was locked into this time, but it was bound to be hare-brained in some way.

At six that evening Miranda pushed open the door to Cafe Trioli and was surprised to see Enid already sitting at a table with two beers, her eyes shining.

"Drink," Enid said, her thick black curls bobbing around her face as she pushed one of the beers across the table to Miranda.

"Hello to you, too!" Miranda leaned across the table to kiss her friend on the cheek. "Now what's so important that I had to drag my butt across town in this revolting peak-hour traffic?"

"This." Enid took a newspaper clipping out of her bag and slapped it down on the table in front of Miranda.

Miranda picked it up and read it over. "Pathways to Pro-tennis Junior Coaching Team," Miranda read aloud. "Join our dedicated coaching team at the Sacramento Tennis Club and mold the juniors of today into tomorrow's pro-tennis champions." She looked up at Enid. "I can't do that," Miranda said, shaking her head emphatically.

"What do you mean you can't do that? You've got to go for it," Enid rallied. "This is perfect for you."

"I'm a low-grade tennis coach at the local club, Enid. This is professional standard, high- stakes tennis. I'm nowhere near their league."

"That's crap and you know it," Enid replied unceremoniously. She took a swig of her beer. "You're a brilliant coach, wasting away in the suburbs with a bunch of tennis moms and pimply kids. You're whiling away the days getting paid worse than a waitress when you could be focusing up and putting your talent to good use."

"But I—"

"No buts, Miranda." Enid cut her off, holding up her hand like a stop sign. "Definitely no more buts. You've got nothing to lose by going for this and it's about time you stepped up to the plate. If you must continue to eat, sleep and breathe tennis, I at least want to know that you're in the best place you can be to do that."

"But I—"

Enid waved her hand again, silencing Miranda. "I said no buts. I've known you since we were thirteen. I've never seen anything more perfect for you." She stopped, tilting her head as she considered her friend. "Let me rephrase. I realize that perfect for you would have been to *be* a tennis pro. But seeing as you got sick and missed your chance," she continued, matter of factly, "this is your new perfect. You can train the up-and-coming players of tomorrow. Now, drink up, my friend. We've got work to do." Enid reached into her bag and hauled out her laptop. Catching the waitress as she walked past, Enid ordered some dips and bread. "We need sustenance. We've got a résumé and a job application to write."

They stayed at the cafe until late that night, compiling Miranda's job history and writing her cover letter.

"Right, I think that's pretty much it," Enid said. "This is as good as we're going to get. So, let's email it off."

"What? Now?" Miranda was suddenly nervous. "Why don't we leave it for a few days and think it over."

"No way, dude. The applications close in a few days. We don't want you to look like you're not organized enough to get your application in on time. We're sending it now." Enid fired up Gmail and passed the computer across to Miranda. "Log in," she commanded.

"Yes boss!" Miranda typed in her login details and together they wrote the email. As Miranda's finger hovered over the send button, Enid pressed her finger down and the email whooshed away.

They looked at each other, eyes wide.

"Well, I guess that's that," Miranda said, taking a deep breath. "I'm sure they won't call."

Miranda was thrilled to receive a phone call a week later inviting her to an interview at the Sacramento Tennis Club.

"What the heck am I going to wear?" she ranted to Enid. "I mean, I'm a tennis coach. All I own are sweatpants and t-shirts. And shoes! Oh my God! Can I wear sneakers to a job interview?"

"You know," Enid began, sounding thoughtful, "if you're ever going to get a girlfriend it might be time we invested in some clothes for you, interview or no interview. You can't walk around in sweatpants for the rest of your life. It's just not sexy."

"Well, I could wear jeans, I guess."

Enid's mouth turned down in distaste. "Jeans are not a lot sexier than sweatpants, Miranda. You can't rely on your good looks and charm forever, you know. I think we should go shopping."

"Oh no." Miranda's heart sank. She hated shopping.

That Saturday she had traipsed around the mall with Enid, awkwardly trying on outfits and rejecting them all out of hand. "This stuff just isn't me," she finally sighed.

"You know, you're right." Enid's eyes lit up. "Let's go to Berkley and find you something a bit more original! Let's go have an adventure."

They jumped in Enid's truck and headed down the Interstate towards the Bay area where it was easier to find something a bit more suited to Miranda's sense of style. Three hours later, armed with a couple of nice blouses that set off her blue eyes and boyish blonde bob, a stylish pair of pants and some retro boots, Miranda was starting to feel a bit more relaxed about her upcoming interview.

The two were sitting in the window of a cafe watching the weekend's afternoon crowds wander past. "Hey, let's go play some pool at Dorothy's," Enid suggested, naming a popular lesbian bar. "Maybe we could find you a hot chick to go with that hot new outfit!"

"Um, thanks, but I don't think it would do me any favors to turn up to the interview with a hot chick on my arm. Anyway, wouldn't…" Miranda paused, searching for the name of Enid's latest love interest, "Dana? Diane? Darlene? be mad if you went to a gay bar without her?"

"It's Debbie," Enid pouted. "And she actually seems to trust me. It's weird. The more she trusts me, the more I want to act like I deserve her trust."

"Hello?" Miranda knocked on her friend's arm, laughing. "Is Enid in there? What have you done with my friend?"

"I know! I'm surprising myself. I've actually been considering falling in love with her."

"Er, I'm not sure you can consider whether or not to fall in love, can you? Isn't it just supposed to happen?"

"Maybe, I'm not quite sure if I'm ready to let it happen though. I'm going to hold off for as long as I can," Enid said.

Miranda looked searchingly at her friend, suddenly feeling serious. "What's happened to us, do you think? Why are we both so scared of love?"

"I don't know exactly." Enid gently swirled the last of her coffee around in the cup, "I guess we've been around the block a bit, haven't we? We've seen what's out there, we know about the heartbreaks and the perils. Maybe it gets harder to convince yourself to take a risk as you get older." She trailed off. "Anyway, all you seem to be interested in is tennis. Girls do get tired of competing for your attention, you know."

Miranda thought about the string of half-hearted relationships she had had over the years, all of which had gradually fizzled out to nothing. Things always seemed to start off well, but then as Enid said, no one seemed to understand Miranda's passion for coaching and the energy she dedicated to her team. Inevitably, the jealousies would arise and then they would drift apart until it was awkward and one of them would have to call it a day. She felt done with that story. "Oh, well. I don't mind being an old maid. It seems sort of romantic somehow."

"There's nothing romantic about being alone," Enid said, fixing Miranda with a long hard stare. "You're going to have to get back out there one day."

"Okay, okay." Miranda put her hands up in mock surrender. "Just not today. I've got enough to worry about with this job interview. Let's focus on one thing at a time!"

It was a nerve-wracking interview and a nail-biting week while Miranda waited to hear back from the club. Finally, just when she had truly convinced herself it had all been for nothing and wondered if she could return the clothes, having only worn them once, she received a call from Jason, thanking her for coming to the interview and offering her a spot on his coaching team. She had, of course, accepted, in happy disbelief.

Walking back across the court to the clubhouse, Miranda shivered in the cooler evening air. She zipped up her sweatshirt and rubbed her arms, hugging herself a little as she hurried up the steps. She knocked lightly on Jason's door and stuck her head around the opening.

"Hey, come on in." Jason motioned her to sit in the chair across from his worn, friendly desk. "Have a good day with the juniors today?"

"Totally." Miranda settled in the chair, resting her elbows on his desk. "These kids are pretty amazing. I think we're going to see some excellent results in September." She wondered again why she was here. They had definitely gone over this just yesterday.

"Glad to hear it." Jason leaned back in his chair and stretched his arms out. "Forgive me, it's been a huge day and I'm beat, so I'll get straight to the point. Jodi needs a proper coaching team now and I want you to have a crack at assistant coach."

Miranda sat up straight in her chair, blinking in surprise. "What? Me? Assistant coach?"

"No, the person behind you. Yes, you, Miranda!" He grinned. "Assistant coach. I'd like to suggest we give it a month's trial and if we're both happy after that time we can make it official. Obviously, it would be a better paid position and we can nut all that out after the trial, but I think we can cross that bridge when we come to it. For now, what do you say?"

"Say?" Miranda looked like she was having troubling hearing him. "What do I say? I say yes. Yes! Wow. This is amazing, thank you!"

"Great! Good." Jason thumped his fist down on the desk with satisfaction. "I feel like this is going to be a win for all of us. I'd like you to shadow me for the next month, watching the match preparations, physio sessions and all other aspects of training. Primarily you'll be Jodi's training partner, hitting balls, matching her across the court, but I want you to be across all aspects of coaching at this level. Tonight I want you to come up with a plan for how you would prep Jodi for the finals on Saturday, and her coming matches over the next month, and then we'll compare your ideas with mine as we go along. I'll get you to make detailed plans for each of her tournaments as well as a general fitness and training regime, and skills enhancement program. You will eat, sleep and breathe Jodi and her tennis for the next month and at the end of it we'll see where we stand. Okay?"

Miranda nodded eagerly and then abruptly stopped, seeing the gangly little bodies and keen faces in her mind. "Yes, coach, it's all definitely yes, but what about the junior team? We've really been building something and I don't want to let them down."

"The juniors will be fine. We've mapped out their game plans for the next few months and the rest of the junior coaching team can carry that forward for now. You'll still be around the clubhouse and you can check in on them regularly and explain to them what's going on. I'm sure they'll be excited for you, and it's good for them to see that we can all advance in tennis, even the coaches. I really admire how much you care, which is why I want to get you up to Jodi's team. I want to focus exactly that kind of passion and energy on getting Jodi that wild card entry into the US Open."

"Well then, I definitely say okay!" Excitement bubbled up inside Miranda. Suddenly she was eager to get going and start on her plan for Jodi for the next few days. Today being Wednesday, she thought, mentally mapping things out, only leaves us two days for last minute finals prep. We don't want to work her so hard that she's tired out for Saturday's match, but we don't want to let her go soft and lose her drive either. She stood up and reached her hand across the desk to shake Jason's hand. "Thanks coach," she said seriously, her eyes shining with focus. "This means a lot to me."

Jason stood too, pushed back his chair and ignored her outstretched hand. He strode out from behind his desk and pulled her into a quick hug. "Glad to have you on the team, Miranda."

He saw her out, calling after her as she danced down the clubhouse steps. "Six a. m. sharp tomorrow morning. Meet us at the Gold River Racquet Club practice courts, where the tournament is."

Miranda looked back in shock and then grinned. "Right on coach. I'll bring the coffee!"

Miranda's cell phone was ringing as she threw her bag onto the passenger seat and slid into the car. Switching to Bluetooth, she fired up the car and waited to hear the beep that meant she was connected through her stereo speakers.

"Hello?"

"Hello yourself," Enid's voice countered. "Where are you?"

"I'm just leaving work."

"Why do you sound so happy? It's late. You know at this rate you may as well give up the lease on your house and move into the clubhouse!"

Pulling out of the club parking lot, Miranda smirked. "Oh, you have no idea."

"What? Seriously, you sound like the cat that got the cream. What's going on?"

"Guess who just got bumped up to assistant coach?" Miranda said.

"Assistant coach?" Enid sounded confused. "I thought you were already head coach for the juniors. Isn't that a demotion?

You know you're supposed to be sad about demotions, not happy Miranda."

"Not if you've been made assistant coach for Jodi Richards!" Miranda said, heading into a long line of evening traffic all trying to go the same way home.

"What? You're kidding me. *The* Jodi Richards? The hot chick who's back after being away for, like, forever from tennis? Miranda Veronica Ciccone, how the heck did that happen and why didn't I know about it?" Enid demanded.

"Okay, okay," Miranda laughed, "hold your fire and I'll explain." She inched the car forward. "Jason used to coach Jodi years ago when she first hit the scene and I guess she asked him to be her coach again for her comeback. I've got a month's trial as assistant coach but I'm going work my butt off and hopefully they'll keep me on. Mostly I'll just be doing training with her, you know, hitting balls back across the court and stuff. But, whatever, I can't believe this is happening. I'm so excited!"

"Wow," Enid said, the glow in her voice matching Miranda's. "I'm so proud of you, Mirry. You want to go get a drink and celebrate at Murphy's?"

Miranda smiled at the sound of her old high school nickname. "I would love to, but I can't. I've got to be at work at 6am tomorrow, with a pre-finals training plan mapped out for Jodi, and at the rate this traffic's moving, I might as well turn around and head there now!" She nosed the car forward another inch, hoping the bumper-to-bumper gridlock would ease up soon. "Do you really think she's hot?"

"Are you kidding? Do you live under a rock? Yes she's hot, she's totally hot," Enid said.

"Oh, well, I guess you're right. Anyway, it's not the point right now. The point is, hot or not hot, I'm her new assistant coach and I'm going to have to get my game plan sorted. Jeez!" Miranda honked her horn, as the car in front of her jerked to a sudden stop. She slammed on the brakes, narrowly avoiding a rear-end collision. "I'd better go, I need to focus on this traffic from hell. I'll call you tomorrow when I'm done and fill you in on my first day of Operation Assistant Coach."

"Ok, be careful out there. Drive safe! Have a great first day."

She hung up and settled back into her seat, enjoying the silence of the car and the settling darkness of the evening. Easing her foot down on the gas, Miranda pulled forward as the traffic slowly began to flow. She couldn't wait to get home and get to work in her notebook.

CHAPTER THREE

At ten past six the following morning, Miranda leaned groggily on the wire fence of the Gold River Racquet Club practice courts, racket bags at her feet and a coffee in each hand, as she watched Jason pull into the parking lot. She had known she would pay for her late night, but she didn't care. She had stayed up conscientiously designing an intricate game plan for Jodi's training. What's one late night, she thought to herself, preparing for the night ahead. After a lengthy conversation with her parents, in which they had peppered her with a million excited questions about her new role, she had finally hung up the phone, promising to call them when she knew more about where she'd be going and what she was doing.

She pored over the match schedule for the next month, noting the court types, the likely player entries, the time between matches, the distance between tournaments, and eventually, she had focused on Jodi herself. She had written an analysis of Jodi's strengths and weaknesses, detailing her areas for improvement, her skills to capitalize on and the techniques they would need to bolster over the coming months. Miranda had drafted a training regime, based on this analysis, and finally, she had tumbled into bed to snatch a couple of hours of restless sleep. It struck her, as she drifted off, that had things been different, had she not had the cancer, all this type of planning could have been done for her. *Oh well*, she thought, wriggling down under the sheet as her cat settled in next to her on the bed, *at least I get to be involved on some level*. In the depths of a dream about Jodi and an endless training formulation, her alarm rudely woke her at quarter past five.

"One of those for me?" Jason called as he approached from the parking lot, eying the coffees.

"Only if you hurry," Miranda replied, taking a sip from one of the cups, "I'm working my way through them."

"Thanks, sorry I'm late," he said, gratefully taking the cup Miranda offered as she fell into step beside him. "I couldn't find my car keys." He shook his head ruefully. "Sally had them in her bag. I swear, sometimes she steals my keys on purpose just to enjoy watching me look for them!"

"If I were your wife I wouldn't be watching you hunt for your keys at five in the morning. I'd be making you sleep in the spare room so you didn't wake me up."

"What are you talking about? You get up at five am too," he said as they walked to the breakout rooms.

"Yes, but if I were your wife, I wouldn't have to. Why oh why did I pick assistant coach? I should have gone for wife," she smirked.

"Ha!" He punched Miranda playfully on the arm. "But then you'd have to be barefoot and five months pregnant, and anyway, I'm not entirely sure you're the wifely type."

"Hmm, yes true, I'm not sure I'm ready for the baby thing, but I will make some girl a great wife one day, you just wait."

"Miranda, I've known you three years and you haven't dated a soul. You need to actually date someone to become their wife."

"Yeah, well, that's your fault," she said, mocking Jason accusingly. "I haven't had the time to date."

"Because coaching the juniors has kept you so busy?"

"That's right."

"Night and day, huh?"

"Yep."

"Not a moment to spare."

"Exactly."

"Well things just got a whole lot worse, my friend. Now that you're on a proper pro tennis team, you're most certainly going to wind up as an old spinster," Jason said.

"I prefer bachelorette, thank you. Spinster sounds like I would have to be very wrinkly, and just because I'm alone doesn't mean I have to be wrinkly and unattractive."

"True. Okay, you can be whatever you want, but hot bachelorette or not, let's make sure we're both coaching a tennis star by the end of this season." Together, they dragged a couple of chairs up to a table against the window at the back of the breakout room. Jason pulled out his folder and spread it open on the table. "How did you go with the pre-finals prep I asked you for?" he asked.

"Really well," Miranda said. She sat down across from him and opened up her notebook. "It's all here. I hope," she added as she slid the notebook across the table.

Miranda watched Jason's face as he read through her plan, hoping to catch a glimpse of approval on his face but his features were blank as he read it over. Her stomach gave a nervous twist as he put his hand on the book and looked up at her. "I didn't expect this much detail."

"Is it okay?" she asked anxiously.

"It's excellent," he replied, suddenly grinning at her. "Your prep plans for the next few days match mine almost exactly. The only thing you've got that I don't have is the backhand training. Explain that one to me a bit more."

"Well," Miranda cleared her throat nervously, "we all know Jodi's got the killer backhand slice, but in a way, that's what people are expecting of her. I thought perhaps we could work on some backhand drop shots so that we keep her opponents guessing. Get her feeling completely confident with a range of backhands. That way, they'll be preparing themselves at the baseline for her trademark slice and she'll surprise them with a shot just over the net. They'll be running themselves crazy trying to catch up with her."

"I love it!" Jason slapped the table enthusiastically, his eyes shining. "Let's pull it all together and we can go over it with Jodi when she comes in later."

Jodi pushed open the door to the breakout room. Two figures bent over a folder in the back corner of the room. Jason was sitting with a woman she vaguely recognized but couldn't place. She studied her for a moment. The woman tucked her short blond hair behind her ear as she leaned forward to point to something on the page they were clearly discussing.

"Ahem," Jodi coughed as she approached them.

They both looked up and Jason smiled broadly.

"Jodi! Excellent, come sit. You remember Miranda?" He gestured to the blonde woman whose full lips gave a warm, if a little timid, smile.

"Yes, of course," Jodi replied, suddenly remembering the pretty, oval face from brief encounters at the clubhouse. "Nice to see you again, Miranda."

"You too, Jodi." Miranda leaned forward, and reached out to shake her hand. "Thanks for having me on your team. I'm stoked to be a part of your comeback!" The warm hand held Jodi's for a brief moment, gave her a light squeeze, and was gone again before she knew it.

"Glad to have you onboard. Have you two been here long?" Jodi drew a chair up to the table.

Jason glanced at his watch. "Gosh, we've been sitting here for two hours!" He stretched out his long arms and gave a loud yawn. "I think it's time for more coffee."

"I'll grab it," Miranda said. "Would you like one, Jodi?"

"I'm all right, thanks. I've already had one this morning. Can't have too much caffeine in this heat—I get dehydrated."

"Of course." Miranda looked vaguely embarrassed, her cheeks slightly flushed. "Can I get you a water or a juice or something?"

"I'm all good for now," Jodi repeated and gestured to the bottle sticking out of her racket bag. "Keeping up my fluids today!"

"Right, cappuccinos for you and me, then Jase. And then I guess we should probably stick to water, too, if we want to keep up with Jodi." Miranda backed away from the table and made her way over to the coffee machine.

As Miranda crossed the room, Jodi noticed her slim, strong figure. She's cute, Jodi thought, contemplating the straight back and long legs.

"How are you feeling after yesterday?" Jason's voice cut through Jodi's thoughts, bringing her attention back to the table.

"Really well." She rolled her shoulders experimentally. "Hardly any pain and the physio totally worked out the residual tension this morning. My muscles feel really free, no stiffness at all."

"Excellent. So I think we've come up with a really strong plan for the next two days, wouldn't you say, Miranda?" he asked, relieving her of the coffee she carried.

"Definitely." Miranda nodded enthusiastically at Jodi.

"Nothing too intense over the next two days, mostly just a focus on some skills training and keeping your body warmed up. Why don't you tell her about the backhand idea, Miranda?"

Miranda's clear blue eyes met Jodi's across the table. "Well, it's just a thought, and feel free to veto it, but I was thinking we could start work on varying your backhand shots, saving the slice for the moments when you really need it, and focusing on some other shots to keep your opponents guessing more on the court."

Jodi studied the earnest face before her. It was a good idea but she felt nervous about any kind of change at this stage in the game, especially coming from someone who had known her for all of five minutes. Becoming predictable, however, sounded a death knell in competitive sports. Jodi looked at Jason to gauge his reaction.

"It's just something we could work on in conjunction with your current training sessions. I've been watching your matches in this tournament round closely, and Jase had me go over a lot of footage from before you, er … " Miranda paused, suddenly going pink. "I mean, from when you were, um … last on circuit," she finally stammered out.

"What about my serve?" Jodi wasn't entirely sure why she was being so cold to this woman but it couldn't be helped. She was fighting her way back onto the court tooth and nail, and if she made it to the US Open, it would be through sheer grit and determination. There wasn't room for protecting people's feelings. And really, the last thing she needed right now was to be worrying about the feelings of some upstart stranger who was trying to turn her game upside down. *Even if she is cute.* Jodi brushed the thought from her mind and turned once again to Jason. She needed to stay focused on the game, and the game alone, if she was going to get anywhere with this comeback.

"I thought we had decided to focus on my serve today, Jase?" she repeated.

"We will, Jodes, but there's no reason we can't add in a little backhand technique to complement your game."

"I just don't want to get myself all confused right now. And I don't want to be second-guessing myself out there, wondering which shot I should play. I want to be able to just go with the flow."

"Of course," Miranda joined in. "And that's the whole point, I guess. If we can build in some extra backhand work you might find you have more confidence to choose between your shots more effortlessly—you wouldn't even have to think about it because the skill would be right there at your fingertips."

"She's got a point," Jason said.

Jodi absentmindedly wound a piece of her hair around her finger, carefully thinking about the proposition.

"Look, I'm happy to check out your plan but really, my main focus right now is to get my serve back up to standard, and then we'll see about building in some backhand work," Jodi said, avoiding Miranda's eyes. She didn't want to be pushed into anything, especially not by a stranger.

If Miranda was disappointed she didn't show it. Jodi was pleased to note she didn't have a princess on her team. Often trainers could become so attached to their own ideas they would push on, just to fulfil their egos, regardless of what their player wanted. She'd seen it over and over and it never ended well. And that's why she loved working with Jason. He always listened to her, and he never pushed. She smiled affectionately at him and pulled her chair up to the table for a closer look at their plan.

"Pretend you're dancing," Jason suggested, as they worked on her service later that morning. "Think of your foot positioning like a dance. Remember the mantra, right foot forward, toss the ball, left leg lift, and down," he said in a singsong voice. "You just need to find your rhythm again, that's all. You're over-thinking it. Cut loose and let your body take over."

Jodi focused her gaze across the court to where Miranda was standing, waiting to receive her serve from the baseline. Her feet were apart and she was rocking slightly, in readiness.

She relaxed her shoulders and tossed the ball into the air. *Left leg lift, and down.* She drove the ball across the court with incredible power, snapping it straight down the service line. Miranda lunged for the ball, and laughed as it clipped her racket and shot up in the air.

"Great serve, Jodi," she called out, "looks like you're really nailing that footwork now."

"Thanks," Jodi called back. "Let's bash out a few more and then hit the showers. I don't want to miss the start of this morning's semi."

Miranda repositioned herself back on the baseline as Jodi lined up for another serve. This time she hammered the ball into the back corner of the service box, again with so much power that Miranda struggled to return it. They rallied briefly before Jodi caught the ball in her hand and set up for another serve. Miranda was holding up well, Jodi noted. Perhaps she would be a good addition to her team after all. *She's certainly better to look at than Jason,* Jodi thought, watching as Miranda bent down to fix her shoelace. Her legs were shapely, and her thin muscular thighs rose up gracefully to meet the line of her shorts.

"Sorry," Miranda called over, as she stood back up. "I'm ready."

Jodi glanced away quickly, bouncing the ball purposefully in front of her.

They kept it up for another fifteen minutes, Miranda working hard to return Jodi's serves, Jodi concentrating intensely on her footwork and positioning, until Jason suggested they finish up for the morning.

"Why don't you ladies get showered and I'll meet you over at center court. I want to call Sally quickly before the game starts."

Miranda followed behind Jodi as they entered the players' locker room to shower. They dumped their bags on benches and Jodi headed to a shower cubicle, towel slung over her shoulder.

"How are you feeling about your serve now?" Miranda asked, heading to the cubicle next to hers. "That was quite a session."

Jodi stripped off inside the cubicle, throwing her clothes over the shower door and slipping her feet into a pair of flip flops. She felt exhilarated from the practice, pleased to feel it all coming together.

"Much better actually. It's surprising how quickly it's all coming back to me. I think it'll be good to start each day on my serve." Jodi turned the taps on and gasped as a stream of cold water hit her warm body.

"Muscle memory, hey. It's a wonderful thing."

Fiddling with the taps Jodi balanced the water temperature and relaxed under the thick spray. "I wasn't sure if I'd still have it, you know? Five years is a pretty long time to be away from a sport like tennis. I'm feeling pretty relieved right now," she said, momentarily letting her guard down. She surprised herself with her honesty.

"I bet. Well, you can definitely feel relieved if that serve is anything to go by. I nearly wrenched my arm out of its socket trying to return some of those balls."

Jodi laughed from inside her cubicle. "Sorry about that!"

"That's okay, you can repay me with soap. I seem to have left mine behind. Have you got some I can borrow?"

"Sure, I'll pass it under."

Their hands met under the wall that separated their showers, and Jodi was suddenly aware that Miranda was naked, with nothing but a thin wall separating them. She shivered, trying not to imagine what Miranda looked like as she soaped her body. Abruptly Jodi turned off her shower and grabbed her towel, rubbing her face hard as if to erase the thoughts.

"Do you need this back now?" Miranda asked, from her side of the wall.

"No, no, I'm done, you can keep hold of it." Jodi quickly dried off and wrapped the towel around her, gathered up her gym clothes and headed into the locker room to get changed. She hurried to pull on her t-shirt, and fumbled with her shorts as she heard Miranda's shower stop. She didn't want to have to get changed in the locker room together. All of a sudden, she felt awkward and self-conscious.

"I'll see you over at center court," she called out to Miranda, stuffing her clothes into her gym bag.

"Gee, you're quick." Miranda sounded surprised. "Sorry, I take forever in the shower. I'll catch you there."

Jodi made a beeline for the door as she heard the latch on Miranda's shower door turn. Glancing over her shoulder she was just in time catch sight of Miranda coming out of her cubicle, wrapped in a towel. Her blond hair was dark from the shower, and her tanned skin appeared soft and steamy. Jodi noticed a long thin scar running down behind her shoulder blade, and quickly turned before she was caught staring, and stepped out of the locker room into the mid-morning heat.

Jodi strode through the grounds towards center court, trying to clear her mind and erase the image of Miranda coming out of the shower, but she kept returning to that scar. What could that be from? So thin, and white against the tan of her skin. Jodi thought again of the towel wrapped loosely around Miranda's torso, catching the swell of her breasts briefly in her mind's eye before she shook her head. Stop it, she told herself firmly. You need to get your libido under control, Richards. How long had it been since she'd been with someone? She realized she and Tara had barely slept together in the last year of their relationship, probably because Tara had been having an affair, Jodi thought.

She flashed back to a night out with friends, just after they had split up. Her friends had wanted to go dancing and she had allowed herself to be dragged along. The lesbian club had been hot and dark and she had gotten tipsy quite quickly. In the darkness she moved to the music, enjoying the sensation of feeling free and numb. In the throng of moving bodies, she became aware that confident hands had found her hips and she turned to find a stranger's face close to hers, their bodies pushed up against each other on the crowded dance floor. The woman's boldness had seemed sexy as she pulled Jodi closer, their bodies moving together in time to the music. Her pulse had raced as the woman lightly kissed her, opening her mouth to let their tongues meet. They had danced like that for a while, kissing and touching in the darkness, until Jodi had allowed the woman to lead her out of the club. Jodi had felt like she was floating as she leaned her head back against the cool leather of the car seat, enjoying the rush of the warm night air through her open window as they drove the dark streets of San Francisco to the woman's house.

In the morning she had crept from the bed and let herself out of the house, onto a street she didn't know. Her head was foggy and her mouth was dry, and a welcome light rain bathed her face, like tears, as she set off on foot to find a landmark she recognized.

That had been almost a year ago now. They hadn't exchanged names, let alone phone numbers or email addresses, and Jodi was glad they hadn't. She didn't need any complications right now—she needed to focus on her tennis. There was no time or space for romance in her busy training schedule, let alone the upcoming tournaments. She had a commitment to give her tennis dream one last shot. She owed it to Nan, and she owed it to herself. And she certainly wasn't in the market for getting her heart broken again. Still, it was hard to completely ignore the undeniable throb inside her as the picture of Miranda exiting the shower came again, unbidden.

The match had been underway for twenty minutes or so when Miranda slipped into the seat beside Jodi in the bleachers, where she sat next to Jason. Miranda's hair was still damp and she smelled of the soap they had shared.

"Got stuck talking to one of the coaches in the locker room," Miranda said quietly, leaning forward to study the play. "Where are they up to?"

"One game all, Kitchfield's serve," Jodi said.

Miranda took out her notebook and began scribbling some quick notes as the play unfolded. Jodi settled back into her seat, feeling safely tucked away under her cap and sunglasses, between Miranda and Jason. The crowd had swelled since the beginning of the tournament. Both of these players were from out of town but the numbers here today were strong. Jodi looked forward to the finals when the crowds would be at their peak. People loved these tournaments and flocked to them from across the country. Between matches, there was live music on the lawns, great food stands, coffee and beer, fun competitions, and of course, nail-biting rounds of tennis to follow through the hot, sunny days.

Jodi glanced at Miranda's hand, resting on her notebook. She studied the neat fingernails and attractively slim, tanned fingers. No ring, she thought. And no ring tan-line. So either she hasn't been in a serious relationship for a while or, she thought, noting no other jewelry except a thin silver chain around her neck, she doesn't like rings. She wondered which it was. Amused at her own curiosity, she turned her attention back to the game.

CHAPTER FOUR

Jason and Sally's lounge room was like a home away from home for Jodi. She had spent many hours here in the past, curled up on the couch watching tennis replays with Jason, staying late to have dinner and drinks when Sally insisted. This afternoon Jason had pulled the curtains so they could get the best effect from the huge flat screen television, while they studied some of Kitchfield's previous matches.

"She's definitely weak at the net. Look how she hugs the baseline." Jason hit rewind so they could watch Kitchfield dive for the ball from the back of the court and miss, one more time.

"See!" he crowed. "Seriously, if you can get in close to the net, you'll totally freak her out."

"I see that." Jodi sighed heavily. "I'm just not sure I'm much better at the net than she is. Now, does anyone want the last piece of vegetarian pizza?"

"Nope, not me, I'm stuffed," Miranda sighed, finishing off the last of her slice.

"It's all yours, Jodes." Jason rubbed his hand over his stomach. "I am definitely done here too." He took a swig of his beer and leaned back on the coach. "I still think we should work on those backhand drop shots. Just so you've got the option. You don't have to use them if you don't feel confident."

Jodi reached over the coffee table and scooped up the last piece of pizza, sliding it onto her plate. She flipped closed the lids to the other boxes and stacked them neatly on the table. "Maybe. We should save these slices for Sal. She might be hungry when she gets back."

"She's always hungry! And, she loves pepperoni pizza now. It's so weird how her tastes have changed since she got pregnant. She used to hate pepperoni, but now she's all over it!"

"Who's all over what?" came a voice from the hall.

"Oh, honey, you're home!" Jason shot up from the couch to help his wife with her bags. "Let me get those. I was just explaining to Miranda and Jodi how you've suddenly developed a taste for pepperoni pizza."

"Did somebody say pepperoni? Thank God! I'm starved." Jason's petite, brunette wife ducked out from under his arm and made a beeline for the pizza box.

"Hi guys. Can't talk. Must eat." She opened the box and took a large bite of the pizza. She groaned appreciatively.

"Hey, congratulations on your win yesterday, Jodi," she said through her mouthful. "How are you feeling?"

"How am I feeling? I feel great. More to the point, how are you feeling? Here, sit down, take a load off." Jodi gestured to the couch.

"Oh, no, if I sit on the couch I need a winch and a crane to get me back off it these days. I like these straight back chairs," she said, dragging a kitchen chair up to the coffee table. "God knows what I'm going to be like in a couple of months. I can't believe I'm this huge after only five months. What are you guys up to?" she asked, taking in the paused image on the television screen.

"We've been watching some re-runs of Selena Kitchfield's matches. She won today's semi and we're analyzing her play for Jodi's match on Saturday. Let me get you a drink, honey. Can I grab either of you guys something?" Jason called over his shoulder on his way into the kitchen.

"I'm fine," Miranda said, as she got to her feet and stretched. "I should be heading home now anyway. I've got to feed my cat before he stages a rebellion and decides to go and live with my neighbor, permanently." She grabbed the used plates and napkins and ferried them into the kitchen. "Do these go straight into the dishwasher?"

"We'll get them, Miranda, just leave them on the bench," Jason said, clearing some space for the dirty plates. Jodi gathered up the pizza boxes. "Sorry to love you and leave you, Sal, I should hit the road too. I need an early night tonight after all the running around we've done today."

"Which direction are you headed, Jodi? Can I offer you a ride?" Miranda said, searching through her bag for her car keys.

"Oh, I'm fine, I'm right downtown. I can easily get a cab."

"It's no trouble for me to drive you. I pretty much go that way anyway."

"Well, if you don't mind, that'd be great, thanks," Jodi said.

"Sorry, it's a total mess in here," Miranda swept what appeared to be a bundle of papers and some clothes from the passenger seat and threw them into the back. "Sometimes I feel like I live in my car! If it wasn't for my cat I could easily forget that I have a house. Just toss your rackets in the back. The trunk's full of training gear."

Jodi's eyes widened as she took in the chaos that was Miranda's car. "It looks like you've been robbed!" She shook her head and found a space for her rackets in the back, then gingerly slid into the passenger seat, primly holding her gym bag since there was nowhere else to put it. A spring stuck into her back and she heard what sounded like papers rustle under her feet as she moved to get more comfortable. "I hope I'm not stepping on something important down here," she said.

"Oh God, sorry," Miranda started the engine, managing the seat belt with one hand and the window crank with the other. The night air was hot. "Don't worry, it's nothing important. Mostly just junk mail and magazines I never have time to read. I bring them with me in the car thinking I might get a moment over lunch or something, and inevitably I end up doing something else and they never get read."

Miranda headed in the general direction of downtown Sacramento. "I can't believe it's still this hot at eight-thirty. We need some rain. Do you want air conditioning? I prefer the outside air but we can put it on if you'd prefer?"

"This is good." Jodi also wound down her window, enjoying the feel of the warm night air on her face.

"So, where to?"

"I'm at the Citizen, near the corner of 9th and J," Jodi said.

"I know it. Have you been there long?"

Jodi tracked back in her head, mentally ticking off the time. "About eight months."

Miranda nodded and they fell awkwardly silent as she directed the car onto the freeway, joining the flow of traffic heading downtown. The air rushing into the car was loud but Jodi didn't want to close her window.

Miranda reached for the radio and pop music filled the car. "Is this okay?" she called above the music. "Want me to search for something else?"

"This is great." Jodi settled back into her seat, enjoying the music and the night sky. She didn't feel like talking and she definitely didn't feel like explaining herself. She knew it must seem strange to be living in a hotel but she didn't care. She felt no burning need to tell her sordid story to this semi-stranger. They had a job to do together and she very much hoped they would manage to do it. That was all.

Miranda glanced at Jodi, her hands resting lightly on her gym bag as they wound through the busy evening downtown streets. She thought she caught a glimpse of sadness cross Jodi's face, but she couldn't be sure. Miranda found herself wondering what would cause someone to live in a hotel for eight months, but she instinctively felt it was not her place to probe. Returning her focus to the road, she felt sure that personal questions would be a no-go zone with Jodi.

Actually, she realized, she hardly knew anything about Jodi. The little she did know she'd heard through unreliable clubhouse gossip and the odd Wall Street Journal report that gave scant personal details. She didn't even know why Jodi had quit tennis, or what had prompted her return for that matter. *Why do I even want to know?* she wondered. *It's not like it makes any difference to how we train now.* She knew it wasn't because of an injury or anything that needed to be factored into training because Jason would have filled her in. At the end of the day, she supposed, it wasn't really any of her business. It's not like she knows anything about me either, she thought. So I guess we're even.

Pulling up outside the hotel, Miranda peered at the tall building, admiring its modern architecture and bright colors.

"Looks like a nice place. Which floor are you on?"

"Twelfth. I'm right at the top," Jodi said.

"Cool, you must get a great view of the city."

"I do, it's especially beautiful at night with all the lights. I like looking down on the city. It's like I get to be a part of all the hustle and bustle without having to get my feet dirty." Jodi's eyes softened as she spoke. She roused herself and got out of the car, reaching into the back seat to pull out her bags.

"Where are you headed now?"

"My place is about twenty minutes from here, down by Stone Lake. I've also got a view. If you lean your head right out the bedroom window you can just see the edge of the Lake."

"People pay good money for that kind of a view." Jodi's mouth hinted at a smile.

"Yes, and I'm one of them. The property tax is astronomical out there! You'll have to come see it some time."

Jodi shut the back door and patted the top of the car. "Yeah, maybe. Well, thanks for the ride. I really appreciate it." Her tone was non-committal, her face suddenly closed.

Miranda shrugged. "Sure, no problem. See you bright and early tomorrow."

"See you then." And Jodi was gone.

Miranda watched the toned, athletic figure walk through the entrance of the hotel, before she pulled away, settling back into her seat for the drive home. She didn't really understand Jodi. One minute she seemed welcoming and friendly, and the next she shut down, as if a curtain had dropped behind those almond-shaped eyes. Something about Jodi made her feel edgy and awkward, like a teenager who didn't know what to do with her hands. Jodi's poise and control unnerved Miranda. Why had she invited her to check out her ridiculous, non-existent view? She grimaced. You're not supposed to do that kind of thing, Miranda, she chastised herself. Now she'll think you're some kind of stalker fan instead of a serious assistant coach. Well, she would just have to clamp down on her friendly gene from now on and show Jodi she was all business.

Recalling Jodi's cool, determined face across the tennis court that morning strengthened her resolve. She'd need to be at the top of her game to keep up with Jodi and provide her with the training partner she needed. It had been years since she'd played any serious competitive tennis and she knew Jodi would expect her to work hard. Miranda was thankful she had taken the time over the years to maintain the skills she had learnt as a junior. If Jodi was going to make it to the US Open, they would need to work as a team and that left no room for embarrassing mistakes. And if Jodi wasn't interested in friendly overtures that was just fine. Switching on her Bluetooth, she punched Enid's number on the speed dial, and settled in for a good long chat.

The following morning, Jason jogged across the court to Miranda and Jodi, who were deciding on the morning's hitting routine. He waved his phone triumphantly in the air. "Guess who I just got off the phone with?"

Jodi's eyebrows rose. "I've got no idea. The ice cream shop? Did they give you a lifetime supply of chocolate? You definitely look happy. Doesn't he look happy, Miranda?"

"That he does." Miranda nodded.

Jason smirked. "I do like chocolate ice cream. But strangely, no, that's not it. It's Dupont, Jodes. They're back on board. I was going to ring them after we saw how you faired in this tournament and convince them to sign you back on for sponsorship, but they just rang me. They want in now!" He punched his fist in the air with his last words.

"Wow! That is good news." Jodi's eyes were wide. "I mean, it's no lifetime supply of chocolate ice cream, but it does mean

I can afford to buy you both at least one chocolate ice cream later." Her eyes twinkled. "Do you like chocolate ice cream, Miranda?"

"Who doesn't?" Miranda grinned, buoyed by Jodi's good mood. Jodi's teasing smile lit up her face in a way Miranda had not seen before, lightening the serious eyes and smoothing the often furrowed brow. Enid's right, Miranda thought, noting the pink of Jodi's mouth and the swing of her long dark hair, which hung loosely about her shoulders this morning. *She is hot.*

"Seriously though, that's brilliant, Jase. Thank you so much." Jodi wrapped an arm around his waist and squeezed.

"Hey, I didn't really do anything." Jason hugged her close. "They rang me! It's happening Jodes. We're going to pull this one off. So, what have you decided for this morning? We don't want you to go too hard today or you'll be tired for tomorrow's final."

"I want to do a bit more on my serve, and then I think maybe we'll give a try to some of those backhand shots you guys having been pushing for. Ready for a hit, Miranda?" Jodi twisted her hair up into a pony tail as she set up on the baseline.

"Sure am." Miranda ducked around the net to get into position on the opposite side of the court. "Serves first?" she called.

"Let's do serves with rallies," Jason directed, lining up beside Jodi on the baseline. "That way we can kill two birds with one stone. Jodi, I want you to try to push Miranda to the back of the court and then move forward to place the ball right at the front of the court. It'll take some pulling off but if you can manage it, you might just have a new signature move!"

They spent the next two hours driving the ball back and forth across the court. Miranda, stretched to the limit, repeatedly threw herself across the court to dive for Jodi's dropshots, trying to keep up with the tennis pro. Just when she thought she would have to call it a day or literally drop from exhaustion, Jason waved her over. "I think that's enough for now, we don't want to overdo it."

Miranda marveled at Jodi, who had barely broken a sweat. Only the slight sheen of moisture around her hairline revealed her exertion in the heat. Miranda didn't need a mirror to know she was red and sweaty.

"Good call, Jase. Much longer and you would have needed to call an ambulance for me," Miranda joked. "Time for a shower. My shout on the soap this time, Jodi."

"Oh, I, um …" Jodi stammered as she packed up her rackets and gym bag. "Thanks, but I think I'll just go straight home and grab a shower there."

"Yeah, right, of course." Miranda felt strangely stung. "Well, if neither of you need anything else from me now, I'll go get cleaned up."

"I think we're done here for today." Jason clapped Miranda on the back. "Nice work. See you back here tomorrow morning. We'll meet in the center court locker rooms at ten."

"Thanks again." Jodi glanced at Miranda and gathered up her belongings. Her eyes held an odd look that Miranda couldn't read, but for a moment she thought it was embarrassment.

* * *

Jodi cursed herself as she slid into the back of the cab and gave the driver her address. She was hot and uncomfortable and everything stuck to her in all the wrong places. What she needed most in the world was a long, soapy shower but she hadn't wanted to go with Miranda. Actually, she *had* wanted to go with Miranda but felt awkward and embarrassed, remembering the sight of Miranda in the shower room wrapped in a towel. The last thing she wanted was Miranda to catch her ogling her like some kind of lecherous lesbian. And the last thing she needed was that kind of distraction.

I'm being ridiculous, she thought, as the cab weaved its way through light afternoon traffic. We shower together; that's what sports people do. It's not like we have to shower in the same cubicle. Jodi flushed at the thought of Miranda without her towel. Oh please, get a grip, she told herself sternly. Tomorrow is the most important day you've had in approximately five years and you're going to blow it by losing focus to some kind of hormonal rush. Miranda seemed sweet and was clearly attractive, but Jodi had no desire to reach out and include anyone new in her life right now.

After Tara, and all the mistakes she had made, she felt done with relationships. She didn't know if it was even possible for her to have a relationship and play the kind of tennis she wanted to play, and right now she wasn't willing to gamble and find out. She certainly didn't want to complicate things by lusting after her assistant coach. No, she needed to concentrate and that was that.

As the cab sped past familiar streets, Jodi reflected on her life. She had her sister, an excellent coach, a small handful of close friends, and was on the verge of resurrecting her promising tennis career. Essentially, her plate was full. There was no room for Miranda on any level other than training partner.

As the cab pulled up to the hotel, she pushed all thoughts of Miranda from her head. She needed a shower, food, and sleep. And she needed to win tomorrow.

CHAPTER FIVE

The ominously dark clouds overhead provided thankful shade. The air was close and heavy with unshed rain, and Jodi mopped her forehead with her wristband. She really needed the rain to hold off. Halfway through the second set, they were neck and neck. What she needed now was to break Kitchfield's serve in this set before the storm broke. She had smashed out the first set, upsetting Kitchfield early on with a few nicely placed net shots that had left her opponent guessing, just as Miranda and Jason had predicted, and now she was fighting with all she had to claim the match. This can be mine, Jodi chanted in her head. This can be mine.

"Fifteen—forty," the umpire called.

So this was it. If she could break Kitchfield's service now, the tournament was surely hers.

Kitchfield stretched high and smacked the ball across the court towards Jodi. Jodi stepped forward, controlling her return to send Kitchfield to the back of the court. They struck the ball back and forth, Jodi keeping Kitchfield at the back of the court as she gradually edged forward. All of a sudden she saw her chance and scooped the ball up, dropping it lightly over the net to land just out of reach of Kitchfield's desperate racket.

"Game: Richards. Richards leads five games to four."

Elated, Jodi looked up into her players' box, seeking out Jason and Miranda. They both wore grins the size of Kansas and were giving her the thumbs up. She had broken service. Now was her chance. She put her head down, reveling in the sounds of the crowd cheering her on as she crossed the court and lined herself up to serve.

Right foot forward, toss the ball, left leg lift, and down. Jodi put all her weight behind the ball and sent it flying into the corner of Kitchfield's service box. Kitchfield flung her racket wildly at the ball and they both watched it spin off over the baseline.

"Out," the umpire called dispassionately. "Fifteen—love."

Kitchfield smacked her racket with the palm of her hand, giving a grunt of frustration.

This is it now, Jodi coached herself. Easy does it, kid. She lined herself up on the baseline again, wiped her palms on her shorts, and gently blew on them to cool them off. Taking a deep breath, she squared her shoulders and cleared her mind. In a flash, she drove the ball straight down the line. It bounced past Kitchfield's racket to land with a thump against the stands and the excited crowd roared as one.

"Thirty—love."

Thunder rumbled across the sky.

Jodi rolled her shoulders, easing the tension out of her muscles and sent another ball flying across the court. They rallied hard, sending each other around the court until Jodi sealed the point with an impossible-to-return backhand slice.

"Forty—love."

Jodi couldn't look up. She heard the crowd as if she were in a tunnel–the clapping, cheering and whistling sounding far away. There was another roll of thunder, closer this time. She looked hard at the ball in her hand, smoothing her thumb over the soft yellow hair, holding it loosely. The world seemed to slow down around her and she relaxed, feeling the first tiny spits of rain prickle against her skin.

Jodi tossed the ball up and gave it everything she had, slamming into the serve with power and determination. Kitchfield shook her head in despair as the ball spun through the service box and barreled past her.

"Game, Set, Match: Richards."

"Yes!" Jodi shouted. She looked up into the crowd, reveling in the wild cheering, and fought back tears. She sent up a silent thank you to Nan as the heavens broke open and the rain began to fall.

* * *

The Gold River Racquet Club sure knew how to put on an after-party. The place was thick with wait staff ferrying heavy plates of food and drink through the dense, rowdy crowd. Pop music blared from an entertainment system set up at the back of the room and groups of people were dancing. Jodi flagged down the waitress as she sailed past and filled her plate with choice, mouth-watering delicacies. She popped one straight in to her mouth.

"Oh, heaven," she mumbled to Jason. "There's nothing like a tiny piece of cheese and pastry when you're exhausted and starving. I think I'll need about five hundred of these to feel full but thankfully they seem well stocked. So what's happened to your sidekick Miranda?"

"She's over there talking with Gabriela Benitez, Sanchez's new coach." Jason nodded across the room and Jodi followed his gaze, spotting Miranda in what appeared to be a fairly intimate conversation with the Hispanic beauty.

"They look like they know each other pretty well"

"I think they're friends. From what I remember, Gabriela and Miranda used to play for the same club when they were juniors."

"Really? I didn't know Miranda played juniors. As in pro juniors?"

"Yep, not for long though. She would have been good, too, but she had some illness and couldn't pursue it."

"We might have been in the juniors at the same time then," Jodi said, wracking her brain to see if she could remember a young Miranda on the circuit from her junior days.

"Maybe, but I think she was a year or so behind you. You were probably on the national circuit by then."

Jodi shrugged. She wondered if Miranda had wanted to go pro. Would she be bitter about an opportunity lost? She certainly hadn't shown any signs of that in the short time they'd known each other. Jodi watched Gabriela lean in towards Miranda, touching her arm as she said something clearly for Miranda's ears only. Miranda laughed and her eyes opened wide as her eyebrows shot up. "If I didn't know better I'd say those two are more than just good friends," Jodi said.

Jason took in the pair. "Nah, I don't think so. Miranda wouldn't know 'more than just good friends' if it hit her over the head at the moment."

"But so, she is, er …" Jodi looked away, suddenly awkward with their conversation. "She's gay?"

"As the driven snow. Just my luck. I decide to become a women's tennis coach and end up surrounded by lesbians."

"Hey!" Jodi punched him lightly on the arm, glad he had lightened the mood with a joke. "Watch yourself, coach man. You're just lucky Sal decided she was straight. I've always had my doubts about her," she teased.

"Me too," he sighed happily. "I still can't believe she said yes to me. And now we're having a baby. I'm going to be a father, Jodi. A fully grown, hairy, manly, muscly father."

"Well, hairy, yes. I'm not sure you fall in to the muscly or manly category."

"Watch it, Richards! I can still take you down," Jason said, lightly bumping her shoulder.

"A fly could probably take me down. I've got no wrestling instincts."

"Well, aren't we just lucky you chose to be a tennis player and not a wrestler then?"

Jodi's gaze wandered back towards Miranda. She frowned slightly as she watched Miranda lean over and take an olive from

Gabriela's plate. "I guess Sanchez would be pretty bummed right now. She didn't even make the semis."

"Not as bummed as Kitchfield. She would have won the whole tournament if it wasn't for you."

"Well, you can't win 'em all," Jody replied brightly, elbowing him playfully in the ribs. "I think I'm ready to get out of here now."

"What? You've only been here for twenty minutes. You can't leave yet. All these people are here to eyeball you, to rub shoulders with America's rising star of tennis!"

Jodi pulled a face. "You don't think you're overselling things a bit?"

"Of course I don't. It's my job to believe exactly that. So just stay another half an hour. Anyway, I want to introduce you to Lisa Sevonny. She's been handling publicity for some of the men's pro-circuit players and I think it might be time you and she had a chat. This could be a good time to start investing in some publicity, get your image up now so we can increase your sponsorship attraction in time for the US Open."

"Whoa, hold up mister! Aren't you getting a bit ahead of yourself there? I've only just made it through the first of three of these tournaments and I've still got to get my ranking back up to somewhere halfway reasonable."

"And that's why I'm here. Yes, I'm your coach, but I'm looking into the future, not just at your game, but at your status as a player. I want playing tennis to be as financially viable for you as possible. I know you hate dealing with the boring old money side of things, but let's face it, my sweet, if you're not floating, we're both sinking."

"True," Jodi tipped her head in acknowledgement. She paused to consider Jason's proposition. "Okay, let's go meet the lady. What's her name again?"

"Lisa Sevonny. And there she is, I'm going to grab her. Stay here. You'll like her. Everyone does."

Jodi didn't get a chance to ask him why that was before he suddenly whisked off across the room. Minutes later he came back, pulling a gorgeously tall, dark-haired woman in an immaculate suit, by the hand.

She smiled warmly at Jodi, her eyes twinkling. "I can usually make it across a crowd without a caveman giving me a tow, but I guess not this time!"

"Jodi, this is Lisa. Lisa, Jodi." Jason waved his hand between them, making the introductions. "Now if you'll both excuse me, I've got to speak with one of the organizers about picking up the trophy," he said and headed back into the crowd.

"It's lovely to meet you, Jodi. Great match today." Lisa's eyes swept Jodi up and down, lowering her lashes. She touched Jodi lightly on the arm. "I very much enjoyed watching you out there on the court."

"Uh, thanks." Was this woman flirting with her? "It's nice to meet you too."

Lisa lowered her voice and leaned in a little closer.

"I was glad you won. I'm going to look forward to watching more of you this season."

Jodi smiled. "I'm glad I won too!"

Lisa laughed. She accepted a glass of white wine from the passing waiter. "Would you like one?" she asked Jodi.

"Sure, I think I could handle a glass tonight." Jodi took a glass, sipping the cool dry wine slowly,

"So, Jason tells me you might be looking for a bit of publicity help?" Lisa said, leaning in slightly. Her glossy her hair swung lightly over her shoulder and Jodi caught the delicate scent of frangipani. "I'd definitely love to work with you," Lisa continued, "It would be easy to raise your profile with a few well timed interviews and appearances. The crowds already love you and we've obviously got a great visual to deal with." Her dark eyes once again appreciatively swept Jodi up and down.

Suddenly, Jodi felt too warm in her long-sleeved shirt. The air-conditioning was working overtime as usual, but under the steady gaze of this confident and charming woman, Jodi felt the room was too hot and she was over-dressed.

Jodi pushed up her sleeves, trying to get some air on her skin. "I guess I am looking for that. I haven't really had much time to think about it, really. Jase just suggested it and voila! Here you are. But it sounds about right."

"Oh, well that is springing it on you a bit! Why don't I give you my card and we can chat about it some more when you've had some time to think it over. I'm happy to email some suggestions, if you like? I can get your email from Jason and put some ideas down for you."

"That'd be great thanks," Jodi took the card and absentmindedly ran her thumb along the edge of the cardboard. "Sorry if I sound a bit vague. Things are only just coming together and I don't have too much of a plan in that department," Jodi said, shrugging apologetically.

"That's okay, I totally understand. Perhaps we could discuss it all over a drink sometime. Maybe somewhere a little less hectic?"

Jodi hesitated. It was just a drink and this was business. "Sure, that would be good."

"Do you …" Lisa paused as if she was not sure she should continue. "I mean, are you free tonight? In a case like yours, the old adage, strike while the iron's hot, certainly rings true."

Jodi tried to get a read on Lisa. It would be good to take advantage of her win at today's tournament. DuPont would like to see her raking up some positive publicity as well, given the renewed sponsorship contract she had just signed.

"Well I've probably had enough wine for tonight, and I promised Jase I'd stick around here for a little bit longer and mingle, but if you don't mind waiting, I could definitely handle a soda later."

"Great, how about I meet you right here by the fountain in 30 minutes or so?" Lisa's smile stretched sweetly across her oval face, showing off her perfectly white teeth.

"Done."

Miranda checked her watch and realized she had been chatting away with Gabriela for almost an hour. It was a relief to find a real friend at an event like this, rather than having to make awkward small talk with mostly competitive strangers.

"I guess I'd better go and find Jodi and Jason, Gab. I don't know if there's any protocol for who I'm supposed to suck up to at events like this, but I should probably check in. I'll come and find you later."

"Let's sneak off later and go get a proper drink some place less snobby!" Gabriela gave her a quick hug, and Miranda chuckled.

"I'd love to, but I'm meeting Enid tonight. Let's catch up another time."

Miranda edged around the crowd, keeping an eye out for her team; she carefully avoided bumping into planter boxes and jostling wait staff as she kept her drink upright.

"Miranda! Over here!" Jason waved her over from beside an open window.

"Phew! It's hot in here." She fanned herself and sipped her soda water. "Aren't you hot in that jacket?"

"Yes, I'm dying, but now I'm too sweaty to take it off," he said, grimacing. "I guess they're having trouble with the air-con."

"Where's Jodi?" Miranda asked, scanning the crowd. "I haven't really spoken to her since the match. I want to congratulate her."

"Last time I saw her she was over by the fountain feature thingy," Jason replied, craning his neck to look over the crowd. "Yeah, look," he pointed, "there she is."

Miranda watched as a familiar woman walked up to Jodi and seemed to ask her a question. Jodi nodded and swung her bag over her shoulder, and they walked together towards the door.

"It looks like she's leaving."

Jason shrugged, raising his eyebrows. "Looks like it."

Miranda watched them walk out the door together, the woman's hand on Jodi's shoulder. She wondered at the odd tightening she felt in her gut.

"Who was that woman?" she asked, trying to sound casual.

"Lisa Sevonny. She's—"

"She's that tennis publicist lady," Miranda cut him off. "I recognize her. My God, she's even better looking in person."

"She is pretty easy on the eye, isn't she! I told Jodi she should speak with her about a publicity campaign. We need to get her profile going now. Strengthen the fan base and get the crowds really jumping behind her again."

"Yeah," Miranda felt strangely heavy. "Good one."

* * *

"Let's go sit out on the balcony," Miranda suggested to Enid, as they paid for their drinks at the bar. "I think it'll be quieter out there. This place isn't usually so busy!"

"It wasn't so busy in the nineties. I'm guessing you haven't been here in a while," Enid teased.

Miranda looked around at the throng of people, crowded around benches, milling by the bar and hanging out by the pool tables. I must be really out of touch, she thought, realizing the once quiet and somewhat quirky little bar had been discovered by the hip crowds of Sacramento. She had loved to go there as a college student, picking a table out on the balcony and losing herself in a book for the afternoon. There would be no quiet reading in this bar anymore, that was for sure.

Miranda headed for the balcony, ducking out through the open French doors; Enid followed closely behind her.

Out on the balcony Miranda scanned the crowded space for an empty table, pulling up short as her eyes came to rest on Jodi, her dark head bent in close across the table with Lisa Sevonny.

"Hey! What're you doing?" Enid exclaimed, bumping into Miranda. "I've spilt my drink all down my arm."

"Shit, I'm sorry!" Miranda turned to help her friend, dabbing the wine off her arm with her napkin. "Um, maybe we should go back inside after all."

"What? No way, it's too loud in there. Look, there's a table right down the side in the corner." Enid pointed to a table past Jodi at the far end of the balcony.

Unable to think of a reason why they shouldn't take it, Miranda headed for the table. Should she stop and say hello to Jodi? She couldn't imagine why she suddenly felt so nervous. You're being ridiculous Miranda, she told herself. Just stop and say hi and move on. It's no big deal.

As she approached the table, Jodi looked up. Her eyes widened in surprise.

"Hi," Miranda said brightly, smiling awkwardly. "I guess we all had the same idea tonight." She paused, not quite sure where to go next, feeling like they were intruding on a private moment. "Uh, this is my friend Enid. Enid this is Jodi, and …"

"Lisa Sevonny," Lisa chimed in.

Enid stepped forward. "I'd shake hands but this one just made me spill my drink down my arm so I'm not sure you'd appreciate the stickiness!"

Lisa laughed and stuck out her hand anyway. "I don't mind. Hello to you both."

"Lisa's a publicist," Jodi said abruptly. "We've been discussing some of the finer points of publicity campaigns. Lisa this is Miranda, my new assistant coach."

"Pleasure to meet you both," Lisa smiled widely. Miranda's stomach felt tight and she edged backwards, bumping a little against the table behind her.

"And congratulations on today, Jodi," Enid said. "I hear you played brilliantly."

Miranda elbowed Enid, nudging her away from the table. "Anyway, we're, uh, just heading to that table over there." Miranda gestured to the empty table at the back of the balcony, spilling a little of her drink onto their table as she did so.

"Oh, god, sorry, second time tonight!" Miranda's cheeks flamed and she dabbed at the table with a napkin, painfully aware of Jodi's dark eyes on her as she cleaned up the spill. "We'd better sit down before I cause any more accidents. Nice to meet you, Lisa. See you tomorrow, Jodi."

Enid nodded goodbye and followed Miranda to the free table.

"Miranda?" She leant forward, as they sat down, trying to catch her friend's eye. "What just happened there?"

Miranda gazed out over the view, shredding the corner of her napkin absent-mindedly, as she avoided Enid's searching gaze.

"Nothing," she said, jutting out her chin with a shrug, "what do you mean?"

"You were all weird. You're never weird. What was that about?"

Miranda finally pulled her mouth in a tight line. "I don't really know. I just feel a bit awkward around her."

"Around who? Lisa?"

"Jodi. She's nice enough and everything, in fact, sometimes she's really nice, but other times she's all cold and proper and I don't really know what to make of her. It seems to be fine if we just focus on playing tennis, but outside of that she's a bit hard to get to know, I guess."

"Yeah, right." Enid paused, her own eyes traveling over the view before them. "It sounds like you might have a little crush on her," she said with a smirk.

"I do *not* have a crush on her," Miranda whispered fiercely across the table, "and can you please lower your voice? She'll hear you!"

"She can't hear me. She's five tables away and we're talking quietly. Miranda Veronica Ciccone. I do believe you've got a crush on your boss."

"She's not my boss and I do not have a crush." Miranda thumped her fist on the table.

"Whatever you say my darling." Enid continued to smirk infuriatingly.

Miranda balled up her napkin in frustration and jammed it into the ash tray. "Let's talk about something else."

"Ok. Like the weather? Shall we talk about what lovely weather we're having? That's a very neutral subject."

"Yes. Let's talk about the lovely weather. I hope it rains. Just on you." Miranda said churlishly, and then suddenly chortled. "Sorry, E., I'm a bit all over the place today. I think I'm just tired. Cheers?"

Enid clinked her glass against Miranda's, still fighting back her smirk, and they settled back to enjoy the evening.

Miranda tried to focus her attention on her friend. But when she stole a glance over at Jodi's table an hour or so later she was surprised to find it occupied by different people. Jodi hadn't said goodbye. Miranda registered a flash of hurt, and immediately dismissed it. It wasn't as if they were friends.

CHAPTER SIX

"Please fasten your seatbelts and observe the no smoking sign for the duration of this flight." The hostess's voice crackled over the loud speaker. "We hope you have a comfortable flight. As this is a short flight, we will only be coming through the cabin once with food and drinks, so we appreciate you having the correct change."

Jodi fastened her seatbelt, tuning out the voice. She had heard these announcements perhaps a hundred times. She raised the window shade, squinting out from behind her sunglasses at the bright blue sky and the glistening black tarmac. In an hour, they'd be in Los Angeles, heading for the Carson Classic Tournament.

She felt Miranda shift in the seat next to her. Miranda had her headphones on and her eyes closed, clearly also attempting to tune out the bustle of the airplane. It had been a whirlwind of a week. They had practiced every day, testing out the new backhand ideas and working on Jodi's serve. Miranda was an excellent rally partner, Jodi had to admit. She was keeping up on the court, which was surprising for someone who wasn't actually playing at competition level. She must have been good as a junior, Jodi decided. Would it be too personal to ask her why she had quit?

Miranda shifted again and her arm brushed against Jodi's over their shared armrest. Jodi left her arm where it was, immediately overly conscious of the light pressure. Careful not to move her arm away, Jodi relaxed into her seat, and gazed out the window, as the plane slowly taxied to the runway, preparing for take-off.

Her thoughts drifted back to Saturday night and she found herself going over the night for the umpteenth time this week. It had ended awkwardly with Lisa. Jodi had begun to sense that Lisa was indeed coming onto her as they sat on the balcony, chatting about tennis and potential publicity ideas. Jodi had felt confused. It was flattering to have a woman as obviously gorgeous as Lisa flirting with her, but she couldn't quite join in the game. Bumping into Miranda had shocked her. Of course, Jodi hadn't been expecting to see Miranda there at the bar, but she also hadn't been expecting the flush of desire she had felt, seeing her looking so cool in snug black jeans and a thin black tank top. The lines and curves of Miranda's body were accentuated by the perfect fit of her clothes, her bare, bronzed skin hinting at what might continue beneath them.

Jodi was used to seeing Miranda in her tennis shorts and sports tees, her hair pulled under a cap. On the court Miranda looked functional and professional and Jodi had been mostly too caught up in her practice to really focus on much except the ball coming back to her. Of course she had noticed the beautifully toned body—how could she not—but they had a job to do on the courts and Jodi was well practiced at avoiding distractions. But she had been unprepared for the raw appeal of the young woman standing before her in the bar on Saturday night. Miranda looked like just the sort of woman Jodi would have wanted to dance with, to buy a drink for, had she been out with friends. Jodi had immediately felt flustered and caught off guard.

Jodi had almost asked Miranda a hundred times during the week about her relationship with her "friend" Enid, but found she couldn't bring herself to mention it in casual conversation. Out of the corner of her eye, she had watched Miranda talking and laughing intimately with the petite and vivacious Enid, even as she listened distractedly to Lisa talk. Heads bent together across the table Miranda and Enid made a striking couple: Miranda with her short blonde bob tucked carelessly behind her ears, showing off her slim, tanned neck, and Enid with her shock of black curls. Jodi decided Jason was wrong. Miranda definitely knew "more than good friends." She had found it harder and harder to concentrate on the conversation at her table, until Lisa had reached across the table and taken her hand.

"I think we'll make a good team, Jodi," she said.

Jodi didn't know what to say. She wanted to edge her hand away but felt that might be rude. Instead she smiled uncomfortably and nodded, leaving her hand awkwardly in Lisa's.

"Gosh," Jodi yawned, using a stretch as a way to subtly free her hand. "It's getting late and I think I've just about hit my limit for today. It's been a huge day."

"Of course," Lisa's perfectly manicured eyebrows pulled together in concern. "You must be exhausted. I'm so sorry, I've just been chatting on and on here."

"No, no, it's been lovely, really. It's probably a good idea for me to get going though. How about I call you during the week to get the ball rolling on some of these ideas?"

"That'd be great, Jodi."

They gathered up their bags and Lisa looked over at Miranda and Enid. "Did you want to say goodbye to your coach?" she asked Jodi.

"Nah, it's okay. I'll see her tomorrow." Jodi was anxious to avoid the confusing feelings of another conversation with Miranda and her potential girlfriend.

"Can I drop you home? It might be hard to get a cab at this time of night."

Jodi didn't particularly want to ride with Lisa. She just wanted to be alone, but Lisa was right, it was going to be a pain to get a cab.

Lisa had chatted easily during the short ride, occasionally brushing her hand against Jodi's as she changed gears, handling her showy sports car with ease. At the entrance to Jodi's hotel, Lisa had again taken her hand, looking into Jodi's eyes with heat and intention.

"It's been great being with you tonight, Jodi. Let's get together again soon, okay? I'll look forward to your call."

As Lisa leant in and brushed her lips lightly against Jodi's, Jodi felt a moment of panic. Lisa's lips were soft and she again caught the hint of expensive frangipani scent.

"Ye... yes, I'll call you from Carson," Jodi stammered, backing out of the car. "Thanks for the, um, ride."

Jodi shot through the revolving lobby door and into the elevator as fast as she could.

Thankfully alone in the elevator she spoke sternly to herself, glowering at herself in the mirror. "What's wrong with you Richards? I'll call you from Carson?" Jodi shook her head and grimaced at herself. Lisa would think she was looking for a relationship at this rate and yes, Lisa was unquestionably good looking, but that didn't mean Jodi automatically wanted to jump into bed with her. In the past this would have been a kind of fun little dalliance, but her focus had shifted now. Her priorities were clear: train, play tennis, win.

The elevator door slid open and Jodi made her way down the quiet hallway with the tastefully dim lighting. She wasn't sure it was a good idea to jump into bed with anyone at the moment. Lisa made a tempting prospect, but there was no real spark between them.

Opening her door, Jodi tossed her bag on the couch and sank down next to it, leaning her head back as she put up her feet on the coffee table. Back in the day she wouldn't have thought twice about enjoying a casual encounter with someone like Lisa, but that had all changed since Tara, and she felt suddenly more protective of herself, like she wanted to be more careful with whom she let come close to her. Unbidden, the image of Miranda coming out of the shower in her towel flashed before her and Jodi felt a jolt in her stomach. "Oh God," she said to herself wearily, getting up from the couch and rubbing her hand across her eyes. "I am not going to be that person."

She went to her bedroom. Stepping out of her jeans, she flopped onto the bed, kicked off her shoes, and pulled up the covers around her. I am not going to be the player with a crush on her coach, she told herself firmly as she pushed her head into the pillow, wriggling into a more comfortable position. I am not going to be that person.

The plane jerked as it hit a patch of turbulence, shaking Jodi out of her reverie and causing her drink to slosh over the edge of her cup.

"Damn," she cursed, mopping it up with her tiny napkin.

Miranda took off her headphones, and watched Jodi try in vain to soak up the liquid on her tray table.

"Here, have mine," Miranda offered. "I don't know why they bother to give out these little tissue things. You'd need a ton of them to actually clean anything up!"

"Thanks," Jodi took the proffered napkin, adding it to hers as she swished it around, trying to absorb the spill.

Miranda reached up and pressed the bell to summon the air hostess. "Enid says you should press the buzzer as often as possible when you're on a flight. You pay so much for the tickets you've got to get added value wherever you can," she said, grinning cheekily.

"How long have you known Enid?" Jodi asked, hoping she sounded casual.

"Fourteen years. We met in the cafeteria in Junior High. She had rice pudding and I had yoghurt and neither of us liked what we had, so we swapped. It was love at first bite, so to speak."

"What can I get you folks?" the hostess asked, reaching up to switch off the call light above their heads.

"Could I grab some more napkins please?" Jodi replied, holding the sodden tissues up as evidence. "I've had a bit of a spill."

"Sure thing, hon. Back in a sec." The air hostess swung back down the aisle towards the galley.

Jodi absentmindedly traced her finger around the edge of the spilt drink. "It's great to have someone in your life that's known you for so long."

"Oh yes, definitely," Miranda nodded emphatically. "Enid just totally gets me, and I get her. I don't have to explain myself and there's never any crap. What you see is what you get and it's always completely and utterly honest. I appreciate that so much."

"That's lucky. I feel that way with my sister. Ally's always been a total rock for me. I just hope she feels the same way about me!" Jodi laughed, wincing slightly. "I know I can be hard work some times."

"I guess we all can," Miranda reassured her.

"Definitely," Jodi nodded. "But Ally's always stood by me, you know? We were really close growing up, and it was just us and our Nan most of the time so we pretty much did everything together. When I lived in San Francisco it was the furthest we've ever been apart."

"I love San Fran," Miranda enthused. "How long were you there?"

A tightness gripped Jodi's stomach as she thought of Tara and the townhouse on the bay. Suddenly she didn't feel like talking any more.

"Five years," she said briskly, saved from having to reveal more by the approach of the air-hostess. She handed Jodi a thick wad of napkins and a fresh drink.

"Here you go hon." She winked at Jodi, gathering up the sodden napkins and dropping them in her trash bag. "Now, if you need anything else, anything at all you just call me, okay hon? My number's written on the back of one of those napkins." She winked again, and sailed off down the aisle.

Jodi shook her head, laughing awkwardly at Miranda's raised eyebrows.

"What can I say? I'm a heartbreaker."

Miranda smiled, her blue eyes unusually serious. "Good to know."

The heat in Carson was intense. The back of the taxi was stuffy, the vinyl seats burning to the touch.

Jodi buzzed down her window, seeking relief from the swampy heat. "Jase said he'll meet us at the hotel later this afternoon."

"Ok. What will you do between now and then?" Miranda asked, checking her watch. It was still early; their mid-morning flight had landed them in Los Angeles before lunch time. Miranda shifted uncomfortably in her seat; her clothes were already beginning to stick to her body.

"I don't know. Check in, have a shower, find some food. The draw hasn't been announced yet but I need to assume I'm playing tomorrow, so I want to take it easy this morning. We'll go over to the tennis center this afternoon with Jase and get in some practice before dinner."

"Would you like me to grab you some lunch? I'm happy to go for a bit of a wander. I'm sure it won't be too hard to find some kind of deli near the hotel."

"Actually, that would be great." Jodi smiled gratefully. "I hate having to search around town for food in this kind of heat, and the hotel food doesn't usually stretch to my dietary requirements. I mostly eat vegetarian, with a little fish for extra protein, but it can be pretty hard to find good quality take out when you're on tour."

"No problem, you just let me know what you'd like and I'll find it. I was actually thinking I might try to find a grocery store and stock up on some supplies. If you want to give me a list, I'd be happy to grab some provisions for you."

"Oh would you?" Jodi looked relieved. "You're a lifesaver."

At the hotel, they peeled themselves out of the back of the taxi, grateful for the bellhop who immediately took care of their luggage. An arctic blast of air conditioning greeted them in the hotel lobby and Miranda actually shivered.

"I never get used to this, even living in a hotel," Jodi said. "They like to keep the lobby freezing cold for some reason. The fancier the hotel, the colder the lobby."

"Well this must be a five-star joint because I'm starting to wish I'd brought my jacket." Miranda hugged herself, rubbing her arms to stay warm.

They were greeted warmly by the desk clerk, who quickly organized their room keys, and welcomed them to the hotel. They piled into the elevator alongside a young bellhop who struggled to maneuver the unwieldy luggage trolley.

"Which floor ladies?" he asked, fingers hovering over the button panel.

"We're both on the ninth floor," Jodi replied, checking their key packets for room numbers. "Rooms 912 and 914," she said, showing the keys to the bellhop.

He nodded and Miranda felt her stomach lurch as the elevator suddenly began its rush upwards.

"Staying long?" the bellhop asked, looking over their luggage curiously.

"Just a few days," Jodi replied, giving nothing away.

"We're over for the Carson Classic," Miranda told him, patting one of their racket bags. "Don't worry, they're tennis rackets, not machine guns," she said. The bellhop grinned, and gave the trolley a hefty shove as the doors slid silently open.

"You're playing in the tournament?" he asked.

"Jodi is," Miranda looked encouragingly at Jodi, surprised to see her give a small shake of her head, a warning frown darkening her brow. "Uh, anyways," Miranda went on, trying to change the subject, aware of a sinking feeling in her stomach. "I don't suppose you could tell me where the nearest grocery store is? I'd like to pick up some healthy snacks and stuff."

"Sure," he said, pulling up outside Room 912. "If you come down to the desk on your way out, I'll draw you directions on the hotel map. There's a great little organic store nearby. They even do take-out meals."

"Perfect," Miranda said, helping him unload Jodi's bags in the hallway. She realized her room was right next door to Jodi's.

"Oh, this is both of us," Miranda said in surprise. "Here, I'll get my bags, too."

Between them they gave the bellhop a tip and when their bags were unloaded they watched him push the trolley away.

"Sorry," Miranda said abruptly, "was it wrong to tell him you're in the tournament?"

Jodi shrugged, hefting her gym bag onto her shoulder. "I just don't like people knowing my business. I get enough of the inquisition from reporters and fans, without adding waiters and bellhops into the mix."

"Oh, of course, I didn't think of that." Feeling like an idiot, Miranda gathered up her racket and wheelie suitcase. "I'll be more careful next time. Um, so just buzz me when you know what you want me to pick up from that grocery store. I think I'll head out in about half an hour."

Jodi thanked her again and let herself in to her room.

Miranda bounced on her hotel bed and gave a little laugh. The room was fancy, adorned with thick dark carpet and tasteful wooden furniture. Having rarely had occasion to stay in hotels, Miranda felt decadent in the luxury of the four-star room. The enormous king-sized bed took up most of the room, made up with crisp, gleaming white sheets and a plethora of plump white pillows. Miranda's cell phone broke out into the opening bars of Footloose and she let it play for a moment before accepting the call.

"Hi Mum," she said, flopping happily back against the pile of pillows. "If I sound different, it's because I'm living the dream."

* * *

A few hours later Miranda stood outside Jodi's room, grocery bags under one arm, knocking on her door.

"Delivery," she called, her voice loud in the quiet corridor.

After a short pause, she heard soft footsteps to the door. Jodi's chestnut hair was rumpled and loose around her face, the telltale lines of sleep creased on her cheeks. She looked delicate, more vulnerable than Miranda had seen her before, standing at the door in just an oversized t-shirt, which hung to her thighs. Catching the line of Jodi's breasts under the thin shirt, Miranda looked away quickly, her pulse quickening.

"Sorry, did I wake you?"

"No, no, it's good. I needed to get up now anyway. Here, come in. I was just having a bit of a recharge sleep."

Miranda followed Jodi into the room, noting a few subtle differences between their respective accommodations. "Where do you want these?"

Jodi pulled on a sweater and took the large brown sacks over to the bar fridge. "Most of it probably needs to go in here, right?" She dumped the bags on top of the fridge. "I'll sort them out in a minute. Thanks so much for getting these for me. How did you go? Did you find the store okay?"

"Yeah, it was easy. That nice bellhop guy gave me directions and it's actually really close by. They've got a super cool sushi bar, too. If we get time we should stop in there and grab some sushi before we leave."

"Definitely, I love sushi."

Jodi's phone buzzed from the bedside table. Scooping it up, she glanced at the caller ID.

"I should take this. Hang on a minute."

Miranda leaned back against the writing desk as Jodi cradled the telephone under her ear.

"Lisa, hey," Jodi said warmly into the phone. "I'm just organizing some food. Can you hold on a tick?" She placed her hand over the mouthpiece. "Is it okay if I fix you up for these groceries later?" she asked Miranda.

"Of course," Miranda replied. "No rush."

"Great, well, Jase said he'd meet us down in the lobby at Two Thirty pm."

"Right," Miranda realized she was being dismissed and took her cue. She headed for the door. "I'll see you down there," Miranda said, and let herself out.

Miranda flicked aimlessly through the hotel guide, barely taking in the glossy advertisements for nearby restaurants and attractions. She wasn't entirely sure what to do with herself. There wasn't time to go back out and do any sightseeing before she was due to meet up with Jodi and Jason, but she felt restless sitting by herself in her room. The luxury she had revelled in earlier seemed impersonal and cold. She was vaguely disappointed to not to have stayed longer with Jodi when she had dropped off the groceries. Somehow she had imagined they would eat together, perhaps have a chat about the tournament to come, and amble down to meet up with Jason. She hadn't expected to spend so much time on her own. *It's just the beginning of the trip Miranda*, she scolded herself. *You should be glad of some down time.* She realized once the tournament began she would be lucky to get a moment to herself.

Maybe she would have a lie-down—she had promised her mom she would get plenty of rest. Ever since the cancer her mom had worried about her health. Was Miranda getting enough rest? Was she keeping up her nutrition? Had she lost any weight recently? No matter how much Miranda tried to reassure her mom, she knew the fear was always there. In reality Miranda was a picture of health. Her physical fitness was the best it had ever been and she was on top of her game. Her six monthly check-ups with the oncologist had been bumped to annual visits a few years ago, and all tests had remained clear since the initial diagnosis twelve years ago, but her mom continued to worry, and the last thing Miranda wanted to do was to cause her mom any pain.

I suppose it wouldn't hurt to rest for half an hour. Miranda had had an anxious night's sleep the night before, nervous in case her alarm didn't go off in time for the morning's early flight. She knew it was ridiculous—her alarm had certainly never failed her before—but she had rarely been on a plane and she tossed and turned for most of the night, intermittently dreaming she had missed the flight or lost her luggage. Yes, a lie down wouldn't hurt right now. It might be the only chance she'd get for the rest of the week.

CHAPTER SEVEN

Miranda fanned herself with the Carson Classic program, grateful for her cap and sunglasses against the relentless heat. She winced as Jodi sent a wide forehand crashing across the court.

"Out," the umpire called. "Advantage Reiner."

The next few moments were nail-bitingly tense as Jodi and her opponent battled for control of the game; Jodi tried to break Reiner's serve while Reiner fought on to defend it. Miranda almost couldn't watch as Jodi won the point and then just as easily lost it again, making awkward mistakes and missing shots that should have been simple for her. Miranda leaned forward in her seat, willing Jodi to pull it together.

"C'mon, Jodi," she heard Jason mutter. "You can do this, champ."

Reiner appeared to be tiring Jodi out. Each woman had chased the other around the court for an hour and a half in a struggle to dominate the game. Jodi had barely managed to take control of the first set but hadn't been able to hang onto her advantage in the second. Now, in the third set, Jodi desperately needed to break Reiner's serve if she was going keep victory within her grasp.

Slicing the ball viciously past her opponent, Jodi pumped her fist in the air.

"Advantage: Richards."

Reiner pummeled the ball across the court, attempting an ace, which Jodi, face pulled tight with determination, returned. Miranda edged forward and gripped the rail in front of her as Jodi and Reiner rallied, sending each other all over the court. The crowd gasped with collective horror as Reiner lunged for the ball and tripped, sliding painfully across the court.

"Game: Richards."

Applause was restrained. The crowd clearly felt sorry for Reiner, who dusted herself off at her bench, gingerly testing her knee for injury.

Jodi rubbed her face with a towel and took a short sip of her drink. Miranda's stomach churned as she noted Jodi's tense, high shoulders and the grim set of her mouth. Miranda wished she could go out there and give Jodi a quick hug to let her know it would all be okay. She looked so painfully vulnerable. Miranda watched the lone figure at the bench, putting herself through some last minute stretching. It took a lot of courage, Miranda mused, considering how long Jodi had been away from the courts. She wondered, not for the first time, why Jodi had left tennis behind. Jodi had claimed to the press that she left for love, but Miranda was fairly sure that whoever had captured Jodi's heart back then was no longer around. She would surely otherwise not have been on a date with Lisa Sevonny.

"Time," the umpire announced, sending the players back to the court.

Jason nudged Miranda. "She's going to smash it now," he said. "Watch."

The palpable tension in the arena hushed the crowd. Miranda's stomach clenched as Jodi sent an ace flying across the court.

"Fifteen—love."

As Jodi crossed to the other side of the court for her next serve, Miranda was suddenly struck by her intense beauty. Her strong, dark features revealed steadfast resolve, and her perfectly toned muscles seemed sculpted under her tanned, shining skin. *She looks like a Greek goddess*, Miranda thought, as an electric jolt of desire ran through her. As Jodi served again, Miranda pulled her attention back to the game. She held her breath as Reiner drove a furious return straight at Jodi's body, forcing her to change position quickly for an awkward return. "Hang on Jodi," Miranda whispered, "just hang on."

As Jodi and Reiner fought on, both players showed clear signs of exhaustion.

"Advantage: Richards," the umpire called. "Match Point."

Miranda's heart was in her throat as she watched Jodi stoically prepare herself at the baseline.

With a grunt, Jodi sent the ball barreling across the court, just touching the net as it dropped over.

"Let," the umpire announced.

Jodi shook her head, obviously frustrated with herself. Summoning up her last dregs of energy, she served a deep, powerful shot. Reiner clipped the ball with the edge of her racket and sent it wildly out of the court.

"Game, set, match: Richards," the umpire called.

Relieved, Miranda cheered and clapped with the crowd as Jodi shook hands with her opponent and crossed to her bench. It had been painful to watch Jodi in such a state. Miranda, emotionally drained, sank back into her seat.

"Well, she's not going to be too happy with that one," Jason said grimly.

"Yeah, she definitely lost it a bit there," Miranda agreed. "What do you think happened?"

"I don't know," he shook his head. "I imagine she'll tell us when this all calms down. Brace yourself for a rough ride tonight. She'll be tough on herself for all those mistakes."

* * *

The mood in the locker room was subdued. "Hey Richards, don't be so hard on yourself," Jason said. "You got there in the end."

Pale and drawn, Jodi leaned back against metal lockers with a blank stare. "I won it, yes, but I could just as easily have lost it. I was all over the place."

Jodi's insecurity made Miranda's heart ache. All the fierce determination from the court was gone and she looked fragile and small. Her eyes were red and Miranda suspected she had been crying. A small vein throbbed at her temple and Miranda fought the urge to reach out her hand and smooth it away, wishing for a second that she could give Jodi a hug and tell her everything would be ok. But they weren't exactly on hugging terms.

"I was a mess. I don't know if I can do this, guys," Jodi said in a small voice.

"But you did do it," Miranda interjected. "You didn't lose. You won, and now you get to let it go. You can move on from this match and focus on making your next one brilliant." She hoped she wouldn't get balled out for speaking her mind.

"Yeah, Jodes," Jason said. "We'll go over the play and work out what went wrong for you, but there's no point getting hung up on it. Miranda's right. Tomorrow's a new day. We need to keep looking forward."

Jodi's eyes moved tiredly between Jason and Miranda. "Okay," she said finally, with a long, tired sigh. "Help me off this bench and into some kind of enormous hot tub and I'll try to forget that I'm really just an insecure blubbering mess pretending to be a tennis champion. If you get me into a bath, I'll get us into the finals."

"Atta girl!" Jason slipped his arm around her and guided her up off the bench. "There's a car waiting for us outside. We'll run you a nice big bath as soon as we're back at the hotel. We can even do bubbles. Miranda, grab her rackets," Jason called over his shoulder as he maneuvered Jodi out of the locker room.

Miranda carefully gathered up the rackets and bags and followed. She wished she could do more to comfort Jodi.

Back at the hotel, after securing dinner arrangements, Miranda went with Jodi to her room to deposit the rackets.

"Want me to get the bath started for you?" Miranda asked as she set Jodi's rackets in the closet.

"Oh, that would be heavenly. Thank you." Jodi sank back on the bed, flinging her arm across her eyes.

"Bubbles?" Miranda asked.

"Yes, please," Jodi answered with a sigh.

Miranda paused in the doorway of the bathroom, admiring the toned, sun-kissed muscles of Jodi's forearm and long, tanned legs. She wondered what it would be like to run her hand across the soft skin of her flat abdomen. With a sudden shiver Miranda turned away, ducking into the bathroom. *I don't know what's got in to me today,* Miranda scolded herself as she bent over the deep hotel bath and turned on the faucet. She suddenly felt vulnerable and exposed, wishing she was back in her own room with her confused feelings. Could Enid be right? Did she have a crush on Jodi? Recalling the last few weeks of training, Miranda realized that she hadn't experienced this kind of emotional intensity since she was a teenager cutting her teeth on the junior circuit.

Miranda tested the water temperature. Winning and losing—almost winning and almost losing—could take people to the craziest heights and the darkest depths. Miranda realized she needed to find her equilibrium again. She had allowed herself to be thrown off balance by all the ups and downs over the last few weeks, but Enid was wrong; there was no crush.

What she needed now was to get back to her room, make herself a cup of coffee, and relax. Later she could phone Enid to debrief. Despite the teasing, she knew Enid had her best interests at heart and would always be there for her. The unquestioning support they gave each other was one of the greatest gifts of their friendship and Miranda was grateful. *Maybe that's why Enid and I struggle to commit to relationships,* she thought, absentmindedly swirling her hand in the bubbles. *Neither of us really needs a partner when we have each other.* She resolved to talk to Enid about it, and to encourage her to try a bit harder in the love department. They had both gotten a bit too complacent when it came to love.

Over the sound of the running water, Miranda heard Jodi's phone in the other room.

"Lisa, hey," Jodi said. "Yeah, it was a tough one."

Not eager to eavesdrop, Miranda quietly closed the door and assessed the water temperature again. *Lisa.* She scooped up a handful of bubbles and blew on them, watching as they scattered back into the tub. Had they been together long? She really knew very little about Jodi's personal life. She knew about the sister, and Jodi had mentioned growing up with a grandmother, but that was it. *Oh yeah, and she lives in a hotel. Why would someone live in a hotel?* She wished Jodi would open up to her a bit more, but Jodi was strictly business, showing up at the courts exactly on time and whisking away directly afterwards. *Probably off to see Lisa,* she thought and then gave herself a little shake. *I almost sound jealous!*

As the bathtub neared full, Miranda turned off the faucet and opened the bathroom door.

"I, uh, I miss you too," she overheard Jodi say. Jodi looked up, startled, blushing deeply under her tan.

"Bath's ready. See you later downstairs," Miranda mouthed. She felt like a stone had settled in the pit of her stomach. Jodi nodded and Miranda slipped from the room, grateful her room was close by as unexpected tears threatened to fall.

"Call me when you get back?" The neediness in Lisa's voice made Jodi cringe.

She took a deep breath. "Sure," Jodi reassured her. "I'll call you when I get back and we'll finalize the publicity campaign, okay?" Jodi tried unsuccessfully to bring the conversation back to business.

"Great. I'll take you for dinner and we'll celebrate," Lisa said.

"Hey, there's nothing to celebrate yet. Don't jinx me!"

"I just know you're going to win this. Break a leg, Jodi."

"Well, we'll see. But thanks. Good night then." Jodi jabbed the hang up button on her phone and tossed it across the bed.

Oh, god Jodi, what have you done? "I miss you too?" What the hell? She chastised herself angrily. She had panicked, that's what. She had tried to say it quickly and quietly but, of course, that was precisely the moment Miranda had come out of the bathroom and she was sure Miranda had heard it.

Great, Jodi thought, *so now Miranda will think that Lisa is my girlfriend.* She rubbed a hand tiredly over her eyes, staring forlornly at the mirror opposite the bed. *It's not like I care what Miranda thinks,* she told herself sternly, but she wasn't quite sure she believed herself.

More to the point, what would Lisa think? *Oh help,* she thought, fighting another round of rising panic. *Lisa!* The last thing she wanted was complication, but she had clearly just done exactly that. *I should have just said nothing, moved on to something else.* Jodi pursed her lips, studying her reflection. It wasn't that easy. She'd always felt awkward, put on the spot even, when people had pressed her for emotional displays and declarations of love. Nan had been so great when she and Ally were growing up, but they hadn't actually said "I love you" a lot. Jodi's dad never really said it, and she could barely remember her mum. She felt out of practice. Tara had eventually become frustrated by Jodi's "lack of romantic spontaneity," as she called it, ultimately labeling Jodi a cold fish.

"Why do I always have to be the one to tell you how I feel?" Tara had whined over a glass of champagne at a romantic dinner gone sour.

"You don't," Jodi placated her, taking Tara's hand in hers over the table. "You know I love you too, you just always seem to say it before me. I'm sorry, baby, I'll make more of an effort, okay?"

"You'd better," Tara had pouted. "You're not the only super-hot brunette in the sea, you know."

Jodi remembered her anger at Tara's thinly disguised warning.

"I'll try to be more on the ball with this kind of stuff." She let go of Tara's hand and picked up her menu. "Now let's order something. I'm starving."

Jodi hated fighting with Tara, and it seemed they had been having more and more petty arguments. Jodi always floundered, unsure of what to say, while Tara always seemed locked and loaded.

"More on the ball," Tara repeated, screwing up her nose like she had smelt something bad. "Still the everlasting, unfulfilled tennis player, aren't you? Even in arguments."

Stung, Jodi had taken a big gulp of her champagne, coughing as the bubbles burned her throat. "Can we not do this please?" she begged. "Let's just enjoy tonight."

"Sure, sweetheart," Tara said with a mean look in her eye. "Why don't you order the gazpacho? Cold soup will go nicely with your icy heart."

The opportune arrival of the waitress had saved Jodi from the need to reply, but she remembered that night painfully. It was one of their last nights out.

Jodi's tired muscles cried out as she eased herself off the large hotel bed and headed for the bath tub. *Relationships*, she thought gloomily. *I'm just useless at relationships. I need to fix this with Lisa before she gets the wrong idea.* She vowed to text her after her bath and clear things up. She really didn't want to drag things out. And anyway, Lisa was quickly proving to be way more intense than Jodi could handle.

Jodi discarded her clothes and slipped into the steaming, jasmine-scented water. Maybe Miranda hadn't actually overheard her telephone conversation. After all, the water was running and she had spoken very quietly. Jodi slipped down into the water, groaning as the wonderful heat worked its magic on her strained muscles. *I need to forget today*, Jodi told herself. *Today was obviously one of those days when things don't come easily. The sooner I'm done with today, the sooner I'll be back to being myself. Whoever that is.*

CHAPTER EIGHT

"Looks like your girl won Carson by the skin of her teeth."
Miranda stepped backwards as an overpowering wave of cologne
assaulted her nostrils. The function room was crowded and
Miranda was jostled as she scanned for an exit. The arrogant and
handsome Craig Simmonds, up and coming men's singles coach,
leered at her suggestively. "Maybe I can give you some pointers
on coaching to win," he said, stepping toward her, "rather than
just scraping by. What are you doing later, Miranda? Wanna get
a…" he paused suggestively, "drink with me?"

Miranda took another step back and bumped into the wall.
Why oh why did she always end up being hit on by the sleaziest
men in tennis, she wondered. Can't they tell I'm a lesbian?
She berated herself for not cutting her hair shorter. These
official tennis functions were starting to become a real bore.
At first she'd been excited by the invitations to proper Tennis
Association dinners, but she'd quickly learnt they were full of
sleazeballs like Craig, keen to show off and make themselves
seem important. At home tonight, as she'd sat on her bed trying

to decide between the yellow or black tank, she had sighed, wishing she could have just stayed in with Eddie.

"That'd be great Craig," she replied diplomatically, repressing a desire to step down hard on his toe, "but unfortunately I can't tonight. Jodi keeps me pretty busy. And Jase really has it covered in the training department. I'm just assisting."

Craig leaned in closer, steadying himself with his arm against the wall and pinning her in. His cologne really was insulting. *Maybe I could give you some pointers in subtlety*, she thought, suppressing a grin.

"There's always more to learn, Miranda." His breath was hot and stale. "I'll take you out one night and I can give you some tips." A tiny spray of saliva jumped from his mouth, his gaze travelling slowly down to her cleavage.

"Miranda, here you are!" Miranda was startled to feel Jodi's fingers wrap around her wrist. She gave Miranda a sly wink as she guided her out from under Craig's arm. "Sorry, Craig, I need her," Jodi said sweetly, blinking up at him innocently.

"Uh, sure Jodi." Craig looked annoyed, his eyes slightly narrowed. "I'll catch up with you later, Miranda," he called after her.

"Sure," she returned over her shoulder, grateful for Jodi's help. "Later."

Miranda let herself be towed expertly across the room.

"I hope that was alright?" Jodi said with a bemused glace back at Miranda. "You looked like you needed rescuing."

"Oh my God yes, thank you so much," Miranda exclaimed, her breath catching slightly as Jodi's hand slipped into hers. "I always seem to get stuck with those kind of guys at these functions."

"I know. It's such a bore." Jodi's hand stayed in hers, "Come with me. Jase said he'd get us a table over by the windows somewhere."

Jodi's warm, firm grip made Miranda giddy. Oblivious to the crowd, she hung on to Jodi, aware of little else but the fit of their hands. *No more wine for me*, she told herself firmly as they moved closer to the windows. *I've clearly had enough.*

"I can't see him," Jodi said, standing on her tiptoes. Their hands still clasped, Miranda wouldn't have been surprised if the whole room could hear her heartbeat.

"Oh, there he is!" Jodi cried, nodding to a nearby table where Jason sat among a crowd of chatty patrons opposite a couple of empty chairs. Just as they reached the table, Jodi pulled her hand away and slid into a chair. Miranda's hand felt instantly empty.

"It's insane in here," Jodi moaned. "Miranda was nearly mauled by that revolting Craig Simmonds, and I can't find anything to eat."

"I know, it's completely painful," Jason replied. "Here, I got you guys these. Eat them up. As soon as the speeches are done, we can leave." Jason slid a couple of laden plates across the table to them.

"Oooh, excellent! Thanks, Jase!" As Miranda reached for the plate, her arm brushed against Jodi's, raising goosebumps on her skin. *What's wrong with me? Why am I so hyper aware of Jodi all of a sudden?* "At least the food is amazing," she said, attempting to sound normal. "I'm starved. I don't know how you do this on a regular basis, though. I thought that guy was going to swallow me whole!"

"Well, my little assistant coach," Jason replied with a grin, "I don't usually have those kinds of problems. Anyway, you're going to have to get used to this kind of crap because it comes with the territory. You lose, you schmooze."

"But we didn't lose." Miranda's perplexed frown revealed her confusion. "Jodi won Carson."

"Yes, I won," Jodi said, her eyes suddenly serious, "but I didn't win convincingly." She absentmindedly popped an olive in her mouth. "I *just* won."

"So we're here to show our faces and let everybody know that Jodi's not spooked and that the Richards train is rolling on into the station. We need to let these USTA people know that she's here and she's in the market for the US Open wildcard," Jason added.

"I see," Miranda nodded. "It's all a bit political isn't it? Sort of an uncharted waters for me."

"Well, stick close by us and we'll guide you through, kid," Jason winked.

"Oh, I plan to," Miranda said, before giving her full attention to the plate of delicacies in front of her.

A series of long and self-congratulatory speeches made by officials of various kinds followed the food, during which Miranda's attention wandered off on more than one occasion. She was just beginning to wonder if things would go faster if she closed her eyes a little when she felt Jodi nudge her gently with her elbow.

"You're not supposed to actually fall asleep at the table you know," Jodi murmured, a hint of a smirk tugging at the corners of her mouth. "We're supposed to be making a good impression."

"Oh, what? I don't think I was sleeping, was I?" Miranda sat up straight, shaking her head and blinking widely. She ran her hand over her mouth, praying she hadn't been drooling or something else hideously embarrassing.

"I think I heard you give a little snore."

Miranda felt her face flush. "I don't snore!" she whispered emphatically. "It must have been Jase."

They both looked over at Jason who was hunkered down in his chair with his arms folded across his chest, trying in vain to keep his eyes open. As they watched, his eyes drooped and his head slipped slowly forward, before suddenly jerking back up, startling himself awake. Miranda snorted a laugh, covered her mouth and pretended to cough; she felt Jodi shake with silent laughter beside her. Jason looked around and caught them. He hauled himself up straight in his seat and glowered across the table at them.

"They really shouldn't serve wine at these dos if they want people to stay awake during the speeches," Jodi whispered.

"What are they even talking about anyway?" Miranda whispered back.

"If you'd been awake, you'd know," Jodi teased. "It's just been all the usual blah blah about the community and the incredible caliber of this year's events. I tell you what, if we weren't sitting all the way across the room from the exit, I would have left ages ago."

"I know. We're kind of trapped over here, aren't we? Why didn't Jase choose a table by the door?" Miranda gazed around her, looking for an alternative way out of the room. "Hey," she said, leaning closer to Jodi. "What about the balcony doors? Do you think we could get out through there?"

Jodi followed the direction of Miranda's gaze.

"I don't know, I didn't go out there, did you?"

"Nope. I was trapped with Craig half the night. I'd be willing to try it though. These guys sound like they'll be going on forever. I don't think anyone would notice if we snuck out those doors from here."

Jodi pulled her purse from under the table and slipped the straps over her shoulder.

"Lead on, Macduff," she murmured. "I can't bear any more of this."

They both caught Jason's quizzical look as they quietly pushed their chairs back, smiling politely at the strangers on either side of them, and slid out from behind the table. Jodi gave Jason a thumbs up and followed Miranda to the side of the room, where they snuck unnoticed out onto the balcony.

"Oh, that was priceless," Jodi whispered, laughing quietly as they stepped out into the cool night air. She eased the function room door shut behind them. "Jase looked so confused. He is going to be so peeved that we left him behind."

"Well, what could we do? He was all the way across the other side of the table. And he was basically asleep anyway."

"I know!" Jodi giggled, leaning back against the balcony railing. "Poor man," her face all of a sudden serious. "He's actually just exhausted, I think. Sal's been struggling to sleep with the pregnancy and he's worried about her so he's not sleeping either. I told him he's not going to be able to help her, or the baby, if he's falling to pieces with tiredness but he refuses to listen."

"That's tough," Miranda agreed, stepping up onto the balcony railing and leaning out slightly towards the view. "Caring for someone can be hard work," she said with feeling. Jodi had the sense that Miranda was speaking from experience, but didn't want to pry. They were both quiet for a moment, each lost in their own train of thought.

"Hey, so I guess Sal will be due in about four months, right?" Miranda asked, breaking the silence.

"Yep, that's the plan." Jodi turned around to gaze out at the view.

"So that's what," Miranda ticked off the months on her fingers, "July, September, October, November. She's due in November?"

"Correct again."

"So what will Jase do then do you think?"

"I imagine he'll take some time off to be at home with Sal and the baby. We'll be ready to take a break from the circuit by then anyway. I'll just keep up some light training until he's ready to come back to work."

"You might be getting ready for the Australian Open by then."

"God, I wish." Miranda could hear the barely hidden yearning in Jodi's voice. "Wouldn't that be awesome? I don't like to think about it though," Jodi added. "Don't want to tempt fate."

"Fair enough."

They both fell silent again, considering the view before them.

"That's probably your hotel over there." Miranda pointed out into the darkness towards a group of tall, well-lit buildings.

Jodi inclined her head to follow the direction she was pointing and Miranda caught the fresh lemony scent of her shampoo as Jodi leaned gently against her.

"Which one?"

"Here, follow my arm." Miranda stepped down off the railing to stand behind Jodi, pointing over her shoulder. "See the big tall building with the red flashing lights?" She let her other hand rest lightly on Jodi's other shoulder, gently facing her in the right direction.

"Um...oh yes, I've got that one." Jodi leaned back slightly into Miranda's arms. She hoped Jodi couldn't feel the sudden racing of her pulse. *What was happening to her tonight?* She swallowed shakily and allowed her hand to drop gently down from Jodi's shoulder to her waist.

"Well, start there, at the tallest building straight ahead" she said, "and then move over three buildings to the right." Their heads were close, cheeks almost touching in the darkness. Miranda shivered at the brush of Jodi's hair against her face. "See, the one with the big blue light on the top. Then go two buildings back," Miranda continued, her voice dropping to a murmur, "and that's your hotel."

"But how can you tell?" Jodi's voice seemed to float through the darkness. Miranda found herself wanting to tighten her arms around her, to pull her close against her. She was intensely aware of the lightest touch of Jodi's back against her chest, Jodi's arm against her arm. Miranda tried to stay very still, not wanting to interrupt the moment by shifting in any way.

"It's the archways," Miranda replied. "Your building has rounded archways over the tops of the windows which make the lights look rounder than the other buildings at night. I noticed them the other day when I dropped you off and thought they would have taken a lot of work to put up." She dropped her arm down on to the railing, no longer needing to point at anything, but neither of them moved away. Miranda realized she was holding Jodi, ever so lightly, in her arms. A breath of wind could blow us apart, she thought. *What am I doing here?* But it was hard to think with Jodi so close.

The balcony doors suddenly swung open and the sounds of the party spilled out into the night. A group of partygoers stumbled, laughing merrily, towards the view.

Miranda stepped back quickly, feeling almost like a guilty child sprung doing something she shouldn't. She stepped back up to the railing, leaving a wide space between them.

"I guess the speeches are finished," Miranda said awkwardly, her heart still beating erratically in her chest.

"Yeah, I guess," Jodi replied quietly.

"Hey!" a nearby voice called as a figure skipped across the balcony towards them. "Jodi Richards? Is that you?"

Jodi swung around towards the voice. Her face broke into a smile of recognition.

"Em! What are you doing here! I thought you were in Florida!"

"I'm back baby," the bouncy redhead replied, flinging her arms around Jodi for a warm hug. "Who's your friend?" she asked, as they broke apart. The woman smiled warmly at Miranda.

"Miranda's just joined my coaching team," Jodi added. "Miranda, this is my friend Emily Hawkins. She used to be the tournament director for the Sun Oaks tournament in Redding and then she ran away to Florida to live in a tropical paradise. Now, what do you mean you're back?" Jodi asked, turning her full attention to her friend. "Fill me in please, what's happened to Stacey? Is everything ok there?"

Miranda's thoughts whirled frantically. *Am I attracted to Jodi?* She couldn't deny the almost palpable connection they had just experienced, but god that would be awkward. She had a job to do. She was pretty sure her job description was supposed to be "hitting *with* the player", not "hitting *on* the player." She shook her head, trying to clear her mind. *This just can't be happening.* Taking a deep breath, she brushed off her thoughts, tuning back in to the conversation.

"Hmm, well, Stacey." Emily was saying, her face twisted in distaste. "Stacey decided there were greener tropical pastures to pursue. She found a horridly young and perky waitress and followed her around like a lovesick puppy until I couldn't stand it anymore and called her out on it. And thus we are," she said, with a pained pause, "henceforth, no longer an item."

"Oh, Em, I'm so sorry," Jodi rubbed her friend's arm, sympathy filling her voice. "That sounds awful."

"It was. And I don't know which was more awful—that she was disgustingly young or disgustingly pretty. Or maybe it was just both. I mean, how can I fight that, right? I'm getting older, it just happens, and I don't want to pretend that I'm not. I want to celebrate my age and enjoy the tiny gifts of wisdom that come with it. I don't want to be one of those women who has to get surgery to stay young in order to keep their partner happy."

"God, no," Jodi agreed, "anyway, you're still completely gorgeous. Stacey is mad."

"Gorgeous yes. Young and perky, not so much. Things are starting to droop a little, if you know what I mean. But you're right. Stacey is mad." Emily guffawed loudly.

"Hey, er, so I might leave you guys to catch up properly," Miranda said, suddenly feeling like a third wheel. "I think I'll call it a night. It was lovely to meet you, Emily. See you Tuesday at the airport, Jodi," she said. Jodi smiled gratefully at her, tucking her arm around her friend's waist. "I'll get my ticket from Jase and catch you there."

"Sounds good," Jodi replied, catching Miranda's eye for the briefest of moments. "Thanks for showing me the hotel."

"Pleasure."

"Now, maybe we should start from the beginning," Miranda heard Jodi say as she headed back into the busy function room. She needed to get out of here. Her heart was still hammering away and the last thing she wanted was to be baled up by any more of the likes of Craig Simmonds. Making her way around the edge of the party, studiously avoiding eye contact, she slipped thankfully out of the front door and into the night. She didn't know what to make of herself. She was clearly overstepping boundaries left, right and center and it just wasn't like her. She was going to muck it all up if she didn't rein herself in now. Assistant coaches do not endear themselves to the pro circuit by developing ridiculous crushes on their players, Miranda lectured herself sternly as she let herself into her car.

Sinking into the familiar seat she laid her head back against the headrest, relieved to be in quiet and solitude.

"Damn it!" she said out loud, banging her palm against the steering wheel. "What the hell are you doing, Miranda?"

She closed her eyes, brushing away hot tears. I will not do this, she thought. This is not on. I'm going to be a professional, and I'm not going to mess up this opportunity.

"So get it together," she mumbled to herself, running her hands through her hair and taking a deep breath. "Just get it together," Miranda said more clearly, resolve coursing through her. Jodi's determined face on the court flashed before her eyes and she sat up straight. I just need to focus on that, she told herself as she started the car and pulled slowly out of the parking lot. Just focus on the tennis and everything else will fall into place.

I can also be very determined.

CHAPTER NINE

"There's a lot riding on this one." Jason's voice sounded concerned on the phone. "Jodi's still rattled from Carson and we need to get her confidence back up."

"But this one doesn't count towards the wildcard right?" Miranda asked, checking the package on her lap one more time to make sure she had all the documents she needed for the tournament.

"Right, but it's still very important. She needs to settle in to winning. She needs to feel like she can do this, because you and I both know she can, and she almost knows it, but she's still a bit shaky."

"Right. I know. We'll be ok, Jase. Try not to worry."

"I know you will." He sighed, clearly frustrated. "I'm just sorry I can't be there."

"It's okay. I'll be here. Now you just focus on Sal and making sure she and the baby are alright. How is she this morning?" Miranda asked.

"The same." Jason's voice was tense. "The hospital has her hooked up to a thousand machines monitoring her and the baby, but they can't seem to work out why she's having the pain." His voice cracked. "It's scary actually."

"Of course it is. Poor Sal." Miranda could only imagine how worried Jason must be. She had seen that worry in her own family's eyes when she had been in the hospital, hooked up to complicated-looking machines that beeped and whirred inexplicably. She had wanted to comfort them, to let them know she was alright, but there were times when she had felt so sick from the chemotherapy, and so weak from the surgery, that she couldn't do much to alleviate their fears. "Keep me posted okay? Let us know how she goes."

"Yeah, of course. Jodi's already asked me for hourly updates. I don't want her worried and focusing on us when she should be focusing on her game. She's got enough going on without stressing out about us."

"I don't think you can help that, Jase. She loves you guys. Of course she's going to be thinking of you. But don't worry, I'll be there to support her and try to help her stay focused."

"You have all the registration papers I sent over? That packet has the passes, the itinerary, the hotels and flights—everything. Everything you need should be in there."

Miranda patted the packet in her lap reassuringly. "I've got it right here. It looks like it's all in order. I'll call you from Texas to let you know when we've checked in to the tournament."

"Great, you can call anytime. If Sal's asleep I'll have my phone on silent so you don't need to worry about waking her. I know you won't need it, but good luck anyway."

"Thanks." Miranda felt a jolt of nervousness. "I'll take it."

Hanging up, she wondered how Jodi was taking the news. She'd be worried about Jase and Sal, but she'd also be anxious about not having her coach with her for the tournament. Miranda would have to pull out all the stops to fill Jase's shoes.

* * *

Jodi tossed her racket bags angrily across the room. "I can't believe I just blew that so badly. I am such an asshole."

Miranda shifted nervously in the doorway behind her. Jodi had been ominously silent in the cab from the tennis center back to the hotel, but it was clear from the deep frown carved across her face that she was not happy.

"Hey everybody," Jodi ranted, pacing the small hotel room. "Roll up to watch the washed up old lady blowing her tennis comeback."

"It wasn't that bad, Jodi," Miranda said gently. "You made some errors, but in general, you actually played really well."

Jodi turned and glared at Miranda.

"Please don't just stand in the doorway," she said coldly. "I don't need the whole hotel to know I'm having a shitty day."

Not sure whether she should leave Jodi to let off steam, or support her through this moment, Miranda hesitated. *Jase wouldn't want me to leave her like this*, she thought, making up her mind to stay for as long as it took, as she stepped into the room and closed the door behind her. Looking about for a place to sit, she chose the writing desk, making room amongst a mess of magazines and papers. She perched on top of the desk, pulling her feet out of the way as Jodi moved erratically around the room.

"What do you think went wrong?" Miranda asked tentatively.

"Wrong?" Jodi glared at her again before resuming her pacing. "The whole thing was wrong, Miranda. I played like an asshole from start to finish. Laurent had me pegged from the beginning—it was as if she knew every move I was going to make, even before I did. I was ridiculous." She bit out the words as she kicked off her shoes and stripped off her socks. "What was I thinking, trying to surprise her with those stupid drop shots?"

Miranda grimaced, feeling responsible. Those drop shots had been her idea and if she was honest, Jodi really hadn't pulled them off today. God, how she wished Jase was here right now to smooth this out.

"It's okay though, right? I mean this one doesn't count towards the wild card points, so it's not like it's all over. And your ranking will still have gone up because even though you lost, you made it all the way to the semi-finals." She tried to come up with something positive to help Jodi shift her focus. "And we can keep working on the drop shots. You'll get there, and when you do, you'll have a formidable weapon to add to your arsenal on the court. You're handling your serve beautifully, and you actually played really well. I guess Laurent just had the edge today."

Jodi sat down hard on the bed, grabbed the pillow and hugged it tightly against her.

"Thank you, but I don't need you to pretend to be all coachy and whisper sweet nothings in my ear here. *I* need to have the edge, Miranda. *I* need to be the one nailing ass to the court and yes, this doesn't officially count, but it counts unofficially, in people's minds—in my mind. I can't be the loser this quickly. I've only just come back. I don't have time to build up a new arsenal. I need to be the winner now."

"You're not the loser and I'm not just pretending, Jodi. I am your coach right now," Miranda said quietly, trying to keep her tone even in the face of Jodi's onslaught. Inside she felt shaky and far from the calm she was projecting. "Yes, you lost this match, but it happens sometimes. You've won all the others and we'll be working our asses off to give you the best shot at winning the rest of them. I believe we can do it."

"Yeah well, I wish Jase were here. No offense, but you don't exactly have the qualifications for this." Jodi pulled off her cap and sent it flying across the room in frustration.

Miranda's jaw was tight. She fought the anger rising inside her. Jodi was right, she was unqualified for this, totally out of her depth in fact, but that didn't mean she had to take any crap. She knew how important this was—hell, if her own tennis career hadn't been cut off at the knees she might have known firsthand just how important this was—and she didn't need Jodi ranting at her to make her realize it.

She let out a sigh, not sure what to do next. She picked up a magazine and rolled it in her hands. Jodi's words stung but she couldn't let her emotions get the better of her.

"You're right," Miranda said eventually, as Jodi stared, stony faced, at the bedspread. "I don't have the qualifications or the experience at pro level, but Jase trusts me and I'm doing exactly what he's asked me to do. I've been speaking with him three times a day, taking instruction from him and following protocol exactly." She slipped down from the desk, feeling frustrated and sad. "I wish Jase were here too, Jodi, but he's not, and I'm doing the best I can to support you. I'm sorry if you feel it's not enough." She leaned against the desk, hoping Jodi would look up. She knew they could get past this if they could just connect, but Jodi steadfastly refused to look up.

Wishing she could walk out of the room, Miranda casually flicked through the magazine in her hands, her eyes skimming over glossy tennis shots and shoe advertisements. While she waited for Jodi to say something, Miranda suddenly realized that she was looking at photos of Jodi: Jodi playing tennis, Jodi in the locker room, Jodi at their training courts, Jodi attending some kind of party, her arm linked through Lisa's. The photos were accompanied by an article and interview, the headline crowning her Sacramento's "Comeback Queen."

"When did you…?" Miranda looked up at Jodi, who finally caught her eye, surprised by Miranda's change in tone. "I thought you didn't like people knowing your business," Miranda said, staring back at the full-page spread. She felt confused.

Recognizing the magazine Miranda held up, Jodi flushed red and hugged the pillow close to her, picking at a loose thread on the bedspread.

"I don't know what I like right now, Miranda," Jodi eventually blurted out. "Everyone's telling me to do this and do that, telling me it will be good for me, good for my image, good for my profile. I'm just trying to stand up long enough on the court to win my matches and not make a total fool of myself, which, might I add, didn't happen today." Jodi's voice raised a notch as she went on, "So I can't really tell you what I *like* right now, but I can tell you I *don't* like it when people like you judge me."

"Oh yes? And what does that mean exactly, people like me?"

"Perfect people," Jodi retorted. "You perfect people who are always so perfect at everything. Well maybe you're not so perfect after all, are you Miranda? It might be best if you just go now," Jodi said flatly. She looked away and fell silent, her words echoing between them like a painful slap.

Miranda carefully closed the magazine and put it back on the desk. Feeling stiff with shock, she walked to the door and put her hand on the doorknob. "I'm sorry I made you feel bad, Jodi. That really wasn't my intention. I wasn't judging you. I was just trying to understand you." She paused, wanting to say more, wishing she could say something to fix this. Her anger was gone, having dissipated as quickly as it had risen. "I'll go back to my room now," she said, as a deep weariness settled over her. "Please call me if you want or need anything." Miranda let herself out of the room, wondering if she was closing the door on her short stint as assistant coach.

Jodi stared stonily at the hotel bedspread as the door closed behind Miranda. She felt shut down, her body tense with frustration. Conflicting thoughts and accusations pulled at her. Agitated, she pushed her hands through her hair, unsure what to do with herself.

"I can't think," she muttered.

The florid pattern of the bedspread suddenly seemed obscene. She hated this cramped hotel room with its old carpet, shabby curtains, and stained light fixtures. She jumped off the bed and pulled the offensive bedspread angrily to the floor, dragging it off into the corner. Beneath the bedspread was a bright yellow synthetic blanket, complete with cigarette burn holes. Jodi felt dirty and alone.

She picked up the telephone and called room service.

A male voice answered. "Your room please?"

"419," Jodi answered.

"What is your order?"

"Can you bring me a bottle of scotch and a container of ice?"

"Uh," the man paused, "excuse me, Miss, but did you say a bottle of scotch?"

"Yes. Can you do that?"

"Well, I guess we can. I'll just have to check with my supervisor on the price."

"That's fine. I don't care what it costs. Just bring it up and leave it outside my door."

As Jodi wrapped herself in a towel she heard a small thud outside her hotel door. She threw on a clean tracksuit and retrieved her order. Drowning her sorrows was not one of Jodi's usual habits, but tonight, in this horrid little room she couldn't face being alone with her mess of thoughts and frustration. She felt like it was just the time for a drink. *Bottoms up, Jodi*, she told herself as she tipped a slug of the amber liquid into her glass and threw it down her throat. She winced at the burning sensation. *I'm sorry Nan. I messed up.* She knew her grandmother would have been disappointed in her. She wouldn't have said much, but she would have given her 'the look': eyes pained, mouth slightly pinched. Nan hadn't needed words to keep them in line when they were younger. She and Ally rarely fought, but if they did, Nan made them feel so bad with her sorrowful look that they made up pretty quickly. Jodi poured another shot and raised the tumbler to herself in the mirror. *To being a sore loser.* She sipped. *There's one title I've earned this tournament.*

* * *

Jodi awoke the next morning to the silent flicker of the television in the darkened room and a pasty taste in her mouth. Her head clanged with pain as she shifted on the pillow and reached for her water bottle, greedily sucking down the water as her temples pounded in protest.

"Oh God," she croaked, looking at the half empty whiskey bottle on the bedside table. She had really done a number on herself.

She switched off the television with the remote and sat up slowly, waiting for the room to stop spinning before she inched open the curtains. As daylight streamed in, she winced and quickly shut them again. Jodi lay back down in the semi-darkness, her body stiff and her head sore, grateful for the black-out drapes. She rolled over and closed her eyes. She needed more sleep.

Some hours later, she awoke feeling marginally better and hungry. She ordered up a plate of toast and coffee, pleased with herself for keeping it down when it arrived.

As Jodi nursed her second cup of coffee and looked out the window at the rooftops of the surrounding high-rise buildings, she allowed herself to revisit the memories of yesterday. Shame flooded her as she recalled what she had said to Miranda. She had felt out of control. Unable to stop herself, the words seemed to run sharply and coldly from her tongue of their own accord. For some reason she had wanted to hurt Miranda, to cut through her perfect, unruffled exterior, and to hurt her like she herself was hurting. *I was a horrible bitch*, she thought. *It wasn't her fault I lost. It was all my own. I should never have blamed her.*

She wondered if Miranda would quit now. Jodi tried to put herself in Miranda's shoes, imagining how it would have felt to be balled out like that and wishing that she had done things differently. *I'd probably leave if that happened to me*, Jodi admitted. *If someone treated me the way I treated Miranda yesterday, I'd tell them to go to hell.*

Jodi knew Miranda had tried to be diplomatic, taking it on the chin in her role as coach, but Jodi also knew that if it had been Jason in that room with her she wouldn't have gotten away with that kind of behavior. *Jase wouldn't stand for that kind of crap*, she thought, as a cocktail of pain and regret mixed inside her. She had taken advantage of Miranda's good nature and inexperience to vent some misplaced anger and she felt horribly ashamed.

She reached for the phone. *I need to call her*, Jodi decided. *Wait, what am I going to say?* She replaced the receiver, resting her hand on it as she stared into space and wondered how to phrase her apology. Jodi remembered the look on Miranda's face as she had ranted, and it cut her to the quick. *I put that look on her face*, she thought sadly.

She needed some air to clear her head before she spoke to Miranda, so that she could say the right things. Jodi decided to take a walk and call her afterwards. She'd suggest coffee. Miranda loved her coffee and she could take her out to a café and apologise to her properly.

On her way out of the hotel, Jodi stopped at the hotel desk to check for messages. When the clerk handed her a folded note, she instantly recognized Miranda's handwriting. As she opened the note, she felt her heart in her throat. Was it a note to say she had already left? Had she gone back to California?

As Jodi scanned the note, relief flooded her; Miranda was at the tennis centre and Jodi should call if she needed anything. She tucked the note in her pocket and walked slowly down the stairs, her eyes sensitive in the bright sunshine. From her note, it didn't sound like Miranda was planning to leave in a huff, for which Jodi felt very grateful. It was better that she had more time, Jodi decided. She would find Miranda when she got back from the tennis center and hopefully by then she would have it all figured out. She would buy her a coffee, explain her behavior and apologize. *Triple decker sundae with a cherry on top*, she thought, smiling ruefully.

CHAPTER TEN

Miranda sat alone at the back of the bleachers, watching the women's finals. Jennifer Laurent was playing effortlessly, winning almost every point as she sealed her dominance of the tournament. Her opponent looked like she was ready to cry as she hung on for dear life to her place in the finals. Miranda's gaze wandered once more around the bleachers, halfheartedly scanning for Jodi among the large crowd of supporters. She didn't really expect to see her. This morning Jodi's phone had been switched off and the 'do not disturb' tab had been hung on the door outside her room. She had felt bad leaving without seeing her, but she didn't really expect Jodi would be calling her any time soon.

Miranda felt a twinge of anxiety as she watched the match, barely registering the play. Would they fire her now? She had let the whole team down. The first tournament she had been responsible for as a coach and not only had her player lost, but now Jodi was holed up in her room refusing to come out or speak to anyone. A complete and utter screw-up, Miranda, she decided, drawing a blank, she considered her next move. Should she call Jase now or wait until she got home? She didn't want to worry him when he already had so much on his plate. She knew he'd be feeling much more relieved now that Sal had been allowed to go home from the hospital but she still didn't want to bother him. It was troubling that they didn't seem to know why Sal had so much pain. Miranda had texted him late last night to let him know the match result and his reply had been short and to the point: *bad luck :-(.*

Luck. Was it luck? Was all this hard work sunk and swum on luck alone? She wasn't too sure. She did know that headspace had a lot to do with it though, and Jodi was definitely struggling to keep her mind calm during the game. *Perhaps when we get back we can do some work on that with Jase*, she thought. If she was still on the team. Jodi had been harsh. Miranda was still smarting from their exchange, but she guessed Jodi had been more angry with herself than with her. Still, her heart felt heavy-laden and anxiety nibbled away at her. Would she have to look for another job? Miranda wondered if Jase would let her go back to the Juniors.

Sighing as Laurent elegantly aced her gasping opponent to win the match, Miranda pulled her cap low over her eyes and slunk out of the bleachers. Laurent was obviously going to be a player to keep an eye on. Miranda wondered why she hadn't seen her at the last couple of tournaments. She'd looked up Laurent's ranking on the internet and found that although she was currently ranked lower than Jodi, she was rising through the ranks quickly. Clearly she was a talented player and would be a challenging match for Jodi. But Jodi could do it. Miranda was confident of that. *She just needs to believe in herself and she can wipe the court three times over with Laurent.* Despite her technical savvy, Laurent appeared to lack Jodi's fire and pizzazz. Miranda wished she could have gotten that across to Jodi. She thought about calling her again but decided against it. She didn't want to seem too pushy, and anyway, if Jodi was going to fire her, she wouldn't mind putting off that moment for as long as possible.

Being unfamiliar with the town, Miranda wasn't too sure what to do with the rest of her afternoon. In fact, it was her first visit to Texas. With limited finances, her family hadn't travelled much. Her parents had never complained or seemed to worry about money, choosing camp-out vacations by the beach (which they had all loved and looked forward to every summer) over expensive plane rides and hotel stays. When she had gotten sick and her medical bills skyrocketed, she guessed much later that it must have placed a huge financial strain on her family, although her parents had never shared that anxiety with her. Miranda had made it a point since then to help out in little ways. When she had begun to earn her own wage, she bought things for the house that she knew they needed. Once, when she found a great last-minute deal online, she sent her parents on a weekend away. She was grateful for the sacrifices they had made to prioritize her health.

Now, scrolling through a webpage entitled "25 things to do in Austin, Texas," Miranda rejected indoor sky diving and other such adventurous tourist attractions, settling on a stroll around the trails of Lady Bird Lake. Some fresh air and clear skies would do her good, she decided, setting out on foot for the short walk to the lake. The late afternoon cobalt sky and shady green paths did little to ease her mounting anxiety, though, and she found herself returning again and again to the situation with Jodi. Frustration and shame coursed through her alternately, as she rehashed their conversation from the night before. She wanted to shake Jodi to her senses —losing one tournament wasn't the end of the world, it wasn't even the end of her career or her goal to win the wild card. It was a surmountable hiccup, a challenge to be met, and an obstacle to circumvent. Surely she was made of stronger stuff? *But I did let her down*, Miranda thought, watching some ducks skid across the big lake. *I let everything escalate into a fight– I should have known how to handle it better.*

Miranda sat down under a tree, glad to be out of the sun for a moment. She pressed her water bottle to her forehead, grateful for the feel of the cool water against her skin. *I let her down and now I just want to go home.* Her cat would be missing her—the house with its hard-to-see view of the lake would be strangely quiet without her. She knew her neighbor would feed Eddie religiously, but would he give him the required cuddles and belly scratches? Eddie wasn't used to her being away and she hoped he wouldn't be lonely. He loved to curl up against her shoulder on the bed, purring loudly into her ear at night. Sometimes she would wake in the night to find him standing over her, batting her nose playfully with his paw.

"No, Eddie," she would mumble, pushing him away gently, inevitably laughing when he would pounce on her feet.

Yes, I want to go home now, she thought forlornly. Heavy tears threatened to spill over, making the lake seem wobbly and blurry.

A little dog trotted down the path towards her, stopping at the chair to sniff her feet. Miranda looked around for its owner, wondering if she could pet it.

"Hi there," she said quietly, reaching down to give the dog her hand to sniff. The dog nosed her warily before giving her a little lick of approval.

"Oh so you'd like to be friends, hey?" Miranda moved off the bench, squatting down next to the dog. She managed a smile as he rolled onto his back and exposed his belly to her for a rub.

"Rub your belly, huh? Well, we've only just met, but okay."

The feel of his soft, warm hair reminded her anew of Eddie and the tears welled again.

"You're a nice boy, aren't you," she told him, tickling him under his chin.

The sound of footsteps on the gravel made her look up. "I see you've met Jackson," a man with a friendly voice said.

Miranda gave the dog a final rub on his belly and stood up, smiling at the man in front of her.

"I told him it might be a bit too early in our relationship for a belly rub," she joked, "but he insisted. I hope you don't mind."

"Oh, not at all," the man replied, grinning at her. "He's terribly easy. I'm constantly finding him on the ground with his legs in the air. My partner Ben and I try to tell him he shouldn't just give it away so easily to strangers but he won't listen to us."

Miranda laughed and choked back a tiny sob.

"Hey, are you okay?" the man looked into her face with concern.

"Sorry, yes," Miranda shook her head, wiping away

disobedient tears. "God, how embarrassing! I'm sorry, I'm fine. I'm just having a rough day." She took a deep, shaky breath and attempted a reassuring smile. "Your little Jackson was reminding me of my cat and I miss him, that's all."

"Oh, I'm not sure we should let Jackson hear you comparing him to a cat," he said. "Have you been away long?"

"No, not really, I'm just having a crappy week." She gave another weak smile.

"Well now! We can't have that. I'm Chris, and you've met Jackson. Would you like to walk with us a little bit until you feel better? Jackson has a lot more peeing to do on particular trees, so if you don't mind stopping every five feet to take note of some kind of excellent smell, we will eventually make it around the lake."

Miranda instantly warmed to him, feeling like some company was exactly what she needed. She missed Enid, and it would be nice to feel like she had a friend. She accepted gratefully and they fell into step on the gravelly lakeside path. Chris was an excellent walking companion, regaling her with hilarious anecdotes about Jackson. He told her about his life partner, Ben, and chattered easily about their wide circle of friends. She, in turn, filled him in on what she was doing in Austin and why she was feeling so sorry for herself. By the time they reached her exit, she felt she not only knew quite a lot about the town and its happenings, but that she had made a new friend.

"Thank you for taking pity on a miserable stranger," Miranda said, shaking his hand warmly. "I genuinely feel a lot better, and now I know where all the best pee smells are at this lake."

"Oh yes," Chris said, lowering his eyebrows in mock seriousness, "any time." He fished in his wallet for his card and handed it to her. "Now, if you need to know where any more good pee smells are around Austin, just give me a call. Jackson has an extensive knowledge of the area."

"Well, I leave tomorrow, but if I ever get back here, I'll definitely call you guys."

"Great! You must come for dinner. I'd like to hear more about all this tennis stuff, and meet your Jodi, too."

"She's not *my* Jodi! And that's if she doesn't fire me today."

"She won't. And if she does, let me know. We'll sic Jackson on her. His growl is far worse than his bite but he can still scare people who are already afraid of dogs. Is she afraid of dogs?"

Miranda laughed, enjoying his sense of humor. "I don't know. I'll be sure to ask her tonight before she fires me."

"Make sure you do that, honey."

She gave Jackson one last pat goodbye and headed for the hotel, enjoying the last rays of the afternoon sunshine.

* * *

Miranda skipped up the hotel steps, feeling lighter with her newfound resolve. *I'm just going to knock on her door and ask if we can chat*, she decided. *I'll apologize for any lack of skill I've shown in coaching and ask her to keep me on as assistant coach.* She felt it was a solid plan—straight to the point, open and honest. If Jodi didn't respond well to that then Miranda was better off back in Junior coaching where she felt confident in her decisions and happy with her performance.

She glanced casually over at the bar on her way through the lobby, wondering if she should order some kind of snack to take up to her room, or wait to see if Jodi wanted to get dinner together. Catching sight of a familiar profile, she stopped. Sitting alone at a table in the hotel bar was the beautiful, poised Lisa Sevonny. Miranda was unsure if she should say hello. As she considered, Jodi approached the table, dressed for a night out, drinks in hand. Jodi looked attractive in tight black jeans and a loose white shirt that showed off her tan and the tone of her arms. Maybe she was a little pale, but certainly the grumpy scowl was gone. *Looks like she's done moping*, Miranda thought. Suddenly realizing that she didn't want to be caught staring, Miranda turned to go, yelping as she crashed into a bellhop. She landed in a sprawling heap on the ground.

"I'm so sorry ma'am," the bellhop cried. "Are you alright? Can I help you?" He reached for her hand and tucked an arm around her shoulders to help her up.

"I'm fine, I'm fine," she reassured him, standing up quickly.

She brushed herself off but pain stabbed at her ankle where she had given it a twist on the way down, and her wrist throbbed. "Really, I'm okay, I promise." She gave him a bright smile as her cheeks flamed red, and limped towards the elevators.

"Miranda! Hey, Miranda!" Jodi's voice carried through the lobby, catching her as she was just about to step in to the lift. She pulled up short, turning to see Jodi hurrying after her through the lobby.

"Oh, hi," Miranda said, hoping desperately that Jodi hadn't seen her crash into the bellhop.

"Hey," Jodi replied, looking at her with concern. "Are you alright? I saw you fall."

Miranda grimaced, tentatively rotating her stinging wrist to test it for injury. "I'm fine. My pride was the worst hit."

Jodi smiled at her hesitantly, her dark eyes uncharacteristically uncertain. "Are you sure? It looked quite nasty."

"Oh yes, nothing's broken except my reputation at this hotel," Miranda said with an awkward laugh.

"Not to worry. Your reputation is more than safe with a fine and discreet establishment like this," Jodi quipped. "Were you going to your room?"

"Yeah, thought I might clean up a bit before dinner. What are you up to?"

"I'm just having a drink in the bar with a friend. With Lisa, Lisa Sevonny— you remember my publicist? Would you," Jodi paused as if unsure of herself, "like to join us?"

"Join you?" Miranda repeated, feeling foolishly caught off guard. She couldn't imagine why Jodi would want her to join them.

"Well, yeah, I mean, if you're not feeling too mad with me from last night." Jodi said, looking sheepish. "I was having a bit of a tantrum last night. I'm really sorry I was rude to you. I got caught up in the ego of everything and I got frustrated and scared. I, well, I hope you can forgive me?"

"Forgive you? Yes, of course," Miranda hurried to reassure her. "I understand you're under a lot of pressure."

"I am, but most of it is self-inflicted unfortunately. I am

working on it, but it does bite me in the butt sometimes, especially when I feel like I'm struggling. Again, I'm really sorry for being a bitch last night."

"It's really okay. I truly do get it. I've been involved in tennis for a long time and I've seen all the different ways stress can play out. It's not the first time I've seen someone get a little steamed up."

Jodi smiled at her gratefully. She tucked her arm through Miranda's and steered her towards the bar.

"So you'll come and have a drink with us then?"

Relief flooded Miranda when she realized that Jodi had no intention of firing her.

"I wouldn't want to intrude."

"You're absolutely not, I'd love you to join us."

Heading back into the bar, with Jodi's arm hooked through hers, Miranda had not missed Lisa's expression of surprise and, she could have sworn, annoyance, as Jodi pulled up an extra chair. Miranda instantly felt awkward, wishing she hadn't agreed to join them. She wondered why Jodi had been so insistent.

"Get you a drink Miranda?" Jodi asked, taking a swig from her bottle of beer as she leaned over the table.

"Sure, I'll have a beer thanks."

"Coming right up."

Lisa took a dainty sip from her glass of wine. The silence stretched as Jodi left the table, leaving Miranda to search for something to say. Lisa leaned back in her chair, treating Miranda to a view of her glamorous profile as she gazed about the room.

"So, what brings you to Austin?" Miranda asked, instantly regretting it. It sounded like she was prying. Lisa arched an eyebrow at her. "I mean, obviously, well, you're here to see Jodi, but was it just… I mean, are you here for long?" she ended lamely.

"Just the weekend."

"Right." Miranda was relieved to see Jodi headed back to the table.

Jodi slid a beer across the table, which Miranda caught deftly. She took a long swig.

"You look like you caught some sun today," Jodi commented.

Miranda's hand flew up to her face, pressing her fingers against her hot cheeks.

"I guess I did. I went for a walk around Lady Bird Lake. It's this giant lake a few miles from here with gorgeous trails around it. Do you know it?"

"I've heard of it but I've never been. I don't really get to see anything when I'm on tour. I'm usually too busy with practice to do any proper sight-seeing. I've got a list though. One day I'm going to go back to some of these places and really check them out. Do some regular tourist stuff."

"Oh, you should," Miranda answered. "I haven't had a chance to travel much, so these last few weeks have been a bit of an eye opener for me."

Lisa gave her a pitying look. "That's a shame, travel is such an education. It really takes you to another level."

Miranda was glad the dim lighting hid her hot blush. She took another long swig of her beer, belatedly realizing she probably should have eaten something before she started drinking.

"Well, you can make up for it now," Jodi said kindly. "We've got a few miles to cover over the next couple of months. Have you been to Canada? Vancouver's next week."

"I haven't, actually. I've always wanted to go there."

"Oh goodness," Lisa interrupted, her face a picture of studied concern, "do you have a passport? You know you need a passport to go to Canada."

Despite her irritation, Miranda smiled sweetly. "Yes I've got one. Enid and I actually went to Mexico a few summers back. I haven't had a chance to travel *much* but I have done a little."

"Wow, Mexico, huh?" Jodi leaned back in her chair, "that must have been fun."

"It was awesome," Miranda replied, smiling as she remembered their whirlwind trip. "I'd love to go back there."

"Oh, Jodi," Lisa chimed in. "You simply must come with me to Maui next summer. Friends of mine have the most divine beach house right on the cliff's edge, overlooking the Pacific Ocean. The sunsets are quite spectacular."

Miranda took another draught of her drink and wondered

whether she should order something to eat or escape back to her room for room service.

"Sounds lovely," Jodi answered noncommittally, sipping her own drink. "I'm hoping to be in full swing with tennis touring next summer though."

"Oh, of course, it's great in winter too. A perfect little romantic hideaway spot."

Just as Miranda was about to push back her chair and make her exit, Jodi's phone rang.

"Sorry, I'll just grab this," Jodi said quickly, checking the display. "Back in a sec."

Oh god, Miranda thought, as she watched Jodi stroll across the lobby, phone pressed up to her ear. *Alone again.* She smiled awkwardly at Lisa, hoping her eyes weren't betraying the dismay she felt.

Lisa's eyes narrowed as she returned the smile. *She's beautiful*, Miranda thought, *but she's hard work to talk to.* She wondered what Jodi saw in her. "Sounds like things haven't been going so well for you in the coaching department," Lisa said casually, looking at her from under long, innocent lashes.

Miranda's chest tightened. *She's beautiful, but she's mean.* She reached for her beer but realized the bottle was empty. She shrugged. "This tournament hasn't been the best, it's true," Miranda replied. "We've been working on some new shots and I guess we've had some teething problems. But I think we can still pull it all together."

"Oh, I'm sure Jodi can do it," Lisa answered, her tone implying that she wasn't so sure that Miranda could.

"I'm sure she can too," Miranda agreed, ignoring the implication. Where the hell was Jodi? She looked over at the lobby and saw her, perched on the edge of a couch with an earnest look on her face. She seemed engrossed in the conversation.

"What Jodi really needs is a serious coach like Jason. I hope for her sake he won't be away much longer. At this point in her career she can't afford to be settling for anything second rate just because she's too nice to say anything."

Lisa's message was clear and Miranda felt a wave of nausea.

Was this what Jodi thought? Was she just waiting for the right moment to let her down gently?

"I need to eat something," Miranda mumbled, rubbing her temples. "Too much sun and now beer on an empty stomach." She smiled wanly at Lisa.

"Jodi and I are going out for dinner soon. I hear the room service is good at this hotel though."

"Yeah." Miranda almost laughed out loud at the obviousness of Lisa's suggestion. "Maybe you can tell Jodi good night for me. I really think I'd better head upstairs now."

"Of course," Lisa replied sweetly. "Lovely to see you again."

Miranda beat it from the table, waving to Jodi that she was leaving as she made for the elevator. "I'm going to call it a night," she called. "See you tomorrow."

Jodi looked surprised but waved in return, as Miranda stepped into the elevator, floating up to her room on the edge of the beer and her empty stomach.

They hadn't mentioned her departure as they sat on the plane the next morning, taxiing down the runway towards home.

"How was the rest of your evening?" Miranda asked casually, thumbing through the airplane magazine as the plane prepared for take-off.

"Fine thanks, just dinner and an early night. You?"

"Same." Miranda replaced the magazine and settled back into her seat. "I didn't have the best sleep though. Think I might try to catch a bit more now." She didn't want to think about Jodi having an early night with Lisa. She couldn't imagine them snuggling into bed together— Lisa seemed too fashionable to snuggle. She closed her eyes trying to find a comfortable spot for her head on the little fold out headrest.

"Here, have my pillow," Jodi offered. "I'm not using it."

"Thanks," Miranda met Jodi's soft brown eyes with her own. "You sure you don't want it?"

"Yeah, I'm going to read my book. You have it." Jodi tucked her feet up onto the seat, her knee pressing lightly against Miranda as she opened her book.

Miranda slipped the pillow under her head and closed her

eyes, instantly aware of the hint of Jodi's perfume from the pillow. She felt the warmth of Jodi's arm pressing lightly against hers on the seat rest, and imagined for a moment they were lying in the same bed. Her pulse quickened and her blood felt thick and hot as she imagined their heads sharing the pillow, bodies casually intertwined. Quickly she pulled the pillow out from under her head and hugged it to her body, shifting in her seat to break the thought. *Please don't go there*, she thought. *Think about something else. Anything!* The smell of burnt coffee drifted up the aisle as the hostesses made their way through the cabin.

Miranda opened her eyes and stared out the window. She would never be able to fall asleep like this. She might as well just have a coffee.

CHAPTER ELEVEN

Jodi stretched out across the bed, freeing her arm from the covers to adjust the pillow. The pull of sleep stayed with her as she felt her body slowly wake. She wasn't quite ready to open her eyes just yet. It felt like morning but it felt early. Could she hear birds? She stayed still, waiting for the faint birdcalls to filter through to her, through the thick hotel glass. That was the problem with living in a hotel. It was such a climate-controlled environment you couldn't rely on the normal signs to let you know when it was an appropriate time to wake up, or go to bed for that matter. The sun didn't stream in through the cracks in her curtains because there were no cracks in these dark and heavy, expensively made hotel drapes. The birds didn't wake her with their incessant chatter because the tinted, soundproof glass kept them at bay.

Still, her body felt heavy and she didn't want to open her eyes; she stayed floating between night and day for a little longer. I should look for a place, she thought as she drifted, dismissing it as quickly as she had thought it, as she had done on many similar mornings in the past few months. Not ready yet. The problem was, she didn't know where she wanted to be. Jodi loved living in the city but it did get a bit claustrophobic after a while, and she loved living further out, where there was space and trees and nature, but she couldn't imagine doing it by herself. So she stayed where she was, waiting for a reason to compel her to move.

Money was really no object. She had invested her previous winnings extremely well due to some sound financial advice, but she mostly lived on the interest of the inheritance she had received at eighteen years old when Nan had died. Jodi remembered the grief she had felt as she sat in the lawyer's office, holding tightly to Ally's hand, while the will had been explained to them. She hadn't listened, not caring what the lawyer was saying, too overwhelmed by the loss of the woman who had raised them like a mother since the death of their own.

The money had been a shock to Jodi and she hadn't really known what to do with it at eighteen.

"You take mine, Al," Jodi said. "I'm no good with this kind of stuff. You have it all."

"Don't be ridiculous," her sister had insisted, "you're keeping yours and you'll be grateful for it in years to come."

"I *am* grateful for it, I just don't want it. I want Nan, not her money."

"Well, honey," Ally gave her a tight squeeze, "we can't have Nan. So do the right thing by her and look after her money. She left it to us on purpose."

When the pain had subsided enough for Jodi to contemplate her future, she had been grateful. Time and time again, it had allowed her to devote her time to training hard, to employing the best coaching teams, to travel to tournaments while she worked on her ranking, and to live with ease while she honed her skills. Thank you, Nan, she silently acknowledged for the umpteenth time, sending a kiss up to the great unknown. I couldn't have done any of this without you.

The rude buzz of her mobile phone broke her reverie and she groaned, burying her head in her pillow for a moment before she rolled over and opened her eyes. "Who is calling me?" she grumbled, stretching out her hand to grope around for her phone. Squinting, Jodi recoiled from the overly bright display in the darkness of her room. Her eyes swam into focus as she saw Jason's name.

"Jase?" Jodi answered with a croak.

"Oh no, sorry, did I wake you? I thought you'd have your phone off if you were still sleeping."

"I guess I forgot to switch it off. I'm awake though. I was just drifting. How are you? How's Sal?"

"Good, we're both great actually. Sal's test results finally came back and she's got a kidney infection so they've given her some antibiotics. Apparently they'll clear up the infection quickly and she shouldn't have any more pain. She's already starting to feel better."

"Oh, that's excellent!" Jodi exclaimed. "Thank goodness. This has been dragging on for too long."

"I know, it's just that they didn't pick it up the first time for some reason—something to do with the protein levels in the urine, but anyway! I'm sure you'd prefer not to be talking about urine first thing in the morning."

"Well, if I have to, I'm glad it's Sal's," Jodi laughed. "But seriously, I'm just relieved she's okay."

"Me too. All this pregnancy stuff is full on."

"I know." Jodi's voice held sympathy. "But you guys are going to be the best parents. And it'll all be worth it when you get your wrinkly, squidgy little baby to hold in your arms."

"I hope so," Jason sounded momentarily doubtful. "What if we get a bad one?"

Jodi laughed, yawning as she sat up in the bed and leant back against the pillows. "I don't think there are any bad ones, Jase. They all come out good. We just make 'em bad."

"Oh well, that's reassuring. Thanks."

"My pleasure, coach man. Any time you need a rousing speech about parenthood, just call me at the crack of dawn. What god awful time is it anyway?"

"It's eight o'clock. I figured you'd be up. Since when do you sleep in anyway?"

"You're right, I should get up," Jodi sighed, swinging her long legs out of the bed. She crossed the room to pull back the curtains. The soft plush carpet felt luxurious beneath her toes. "So what can I do for you? Early morning chat about pee and parenting or something else?"

"Something else. Why is Lisa Sevonny emailing through promotional plans to me? I thought we decided you were going to deal with that?"

"Oh, right," Jodi groaned, and leaned her head against the thick hotel window as she stared down at the pavement from twelve stories up. The little people below were all determinedly going about their businesses, oblivious to her dark brown eyes.

"It's all gotten complicated," Jodi said eventually

"Hmm. Want to talk about it?"

Jodi pursed her lips. "Yes, I guess."

"Did something happen in Austin? Lisa's email was weird. She mentions seeing you in Austin but then sent all the details to me. What was Lisa doing in Austin?"

"Well…I guess that's where it gets complicated." Jodi tracked back in her head, unsure where to start, suddenly shy to talk with Jase about the personal details of her life. She unexpectedly knew this was important. This was where she had gone wrong last time. She hadn't shared anything with him. *He tells me all about his life and I shut up tight like a kid who just got braces,* she thought ruefully.

"After you introduced us at the party at Gold River," Jodi began, "we went for a drink. I thought we were just going to chat about the promo stuff but when she dropped me home, well…er, she kissed me."

"What?" Jason spluttered down the line. "I mean, um, was that okay with you?"

Jodi took a deep breath. "It was fine. I can handle myself, Jase. Well, mostly anyway. I didn't mind that she'd kissed me, but I didn't want her to get the wrong idea. Then she called me in Carson and I thought we were just chatting about publicity and all of a sudden she told me she missed me and I stupidly told her I missed her too." The words tumbled out as Jodi turned away from the window to pace around the room. "And I didn't. I didn't miss her at all, but it got awkward and I didn't know what to say, so I said I did."

"Right." Jason drew out the word. "I can see how that works."

"Well, then I lost in Austin," Jodi went on, ignoring his sarcasm, "and I felt shitty and Lisa just turned up! I didn't know what to do, you know?"

"Tell her you missed her again?" Jason suggested.

"Whatever. So then I was horribly rude to Miranda and God only knows what she thinks of me now, she probably hates me, but I somehow orchestrated us all to have a drink and then I bailed and left them together, and Miranda ran away." Jodi gave a hollow laugh. "I told Lisa to email the details of the campaign through to you and begged off the rest of the night with a headache. I'm surprised she sent the campaign through to you at all."

"Ah." She could almost hear Jason grinning down the line. "It sounds like you've handled everything excellently. If it's any consolation, Lisa told me she had been surprised to 'bump into you' in Austin, so she's at least acting as if she's playing it casual."

"That's a relief. I tried bringing it back to business but I really shouldn't have told her I missed her. She put me on the spot and I instantly caved. I'm such a loser like that."

"Hey, please don't talk about my star tennis player like that," Jason said gently, "not to mention my friend. You're not a loser. It's hard when people catch you off guard."

"Thanks, Jase." Jodi felt relieved to have his support.

"So what happened with Miranda? Why might she hate you now? She didn't mention that when I spoke to her this morning, but then, I didn't ask her either."

"My God Jase, what time did you ring her? If it's only eight o'clock now—"

"I called her at seven," he said, cutting Jodi off. "She's worked for me for a while now. She's used to it. So what did you do to her? I did wonder why she sounded a bit wary about everything."

"Oh, I was a royal bitch. I was sore about losing and I took it out on her. You know how I can be sometimes. She was nice about it later when I apologized, but I'd be upset if I were her."

"I think I know what you mean. Want me to talk to her?"

Jodi hesitated, sitting down on the bed. "I don't know. I don't think so. I apologized and I did try to explain. It's probably best to just leave it now."

"Okay, if you change your mind, just let me know. So, what do you want me to do with Lisa's publicity campaign?"

"Send it to me. I'll check it out. Sorry, I should have just got her to send it to me in the first place but I needed to head her off a bit."

"No problem. That's what I'm here for." Jason paused, shifting gears. "Now, what are we going to do with this next week? We've got eight days before Vancouver and we need to make every second count."

CHAPTER TWELVE

Miranda turned her face up to the sun, closing her eyes as she sat on her back step, basking in the early morning warmth. The back door into her little kitchen was open behind her and she leaned against the doorframe. In her hand, she cradled a cup of tea, enjoying the fragrance of the brew as much as the taste. Eddie rolled lazily onto his belly and she dropped a hand down to him, smiling as he pushed his face into her palm.

"I missed you too," she said, giving him a scooch under the chin. "What shall we do today?" she asked him, gently pulling his ears. He answered by trapping her hand between his paws and giving her a couple of licks, followed by a sudden nip.

"Hey!" Miranda cried in mock outrage. "No biting please, mister." She retracted her hand from his jaws and resumed tickling his belly. "I think we need to do some weeding out here." She ran her eye over the small garden. "This yard is a mess. What were you doing while I was away? You've let the place go to wrack and ruin," she scolded.

Weeds had shot up amongst her herbs and veggies, vying for prominence. Her little patch of lawn was dotted with wildflowers, the grass having grown higher than usual in the warm summer weather. A passion fruit vine, bursting with exotic white flowers and dark black fruit, tangled its way along the back fence, pulling the trellis she had erected away. She loved her little private garden and spent hours puttering in amongst the greenery whenever she could.

Eddie rolled over and stood up haughtily, flicking his tail in the air as he wandered away. He deliberately sat down just out of her reach.

Miranda rested her teacup on the stoop and stood up, lazily stretching her arms up to the sky. Her shirt rose up, exposing her taught midriff and she ran her hand over the bare skin. It was good to be home. She could go for a run today. And get a coffee with Enid. Actually, maybe Enid could visit her here. She didn't feel like going far. Lately she'd spent way too much time away from her little palace with the hard-to-reach view of the lake.

Squatting down next to her herb patch, she pulled out dandelions and other stray weeds from the tangled array of plants. The thick brown earth was already warming up, and it stuck to her fingers as she unearthed the offending intruders. She broke off a leaf of basil and popped it in her mouth, instantly thinking of pizza as she chewed. She planned to savor these couple of days to herself. She would move slowly, enjoy some quiet and calm space, free from the pressures of tennis and the whirlwind of emotions that surrounded Jodi.

It's time to get it together now, she told herself sternly. You were unglued in Austin. Well, it's not like it didn't have its challenges, she thought, grimacing as memories of their trip washed over her. It had felt like a disaster from start to finish. Jodi's loss to Laurent, their fight, the awkward drinks in the bar with Lisa—Miranda could only call that trip an epic fail.

Enid sat cross-legged on the bed, while Miranda perched on the window seat, leaning her head out the window to look at the lake. The old brick house was skinny and tall, like a rickety old lady, Miranda sometimes thought. Her bedroom was perched at the top of a wobbly old wooden staircase. The taps were worn and the pipes juddered when you turned on the hot water, but the light was good and the house was airy, with lots of great big rattily windows to throw open.

"Careful you don't fall out," Enid cautioned as Miranda stretched further out the window.

"You always say that."

"And you always nearly fall out. So be careful, would you?"

"Okay, okay." Miranda pulled her head back in the window and leaned back against the frame, looking over at her friend.

"So, what I'm hearing from you is that you messed it all up?" Enid said, extending her legs across the soft cotton bedspread. Afternoon sunlight spilled into the room, adding an extra glow to the light yellow walls.

"I'd say that's pretty much it, yes," Miranda grimaced.

"And now you don't know if Jodi's just being too polite to fire you? I doubt that would be the case. From what I know of these tennis stars, they aren't too shy to ask for what they want. And anyway, she probably wouldn't fire you herself. She'd get Jason to do it. And that wouldn't be hard; you're on probation as assistant coach anyway, right?"

"Right, thanks for reminding me. But where exactly do you get your in-depth knowledge of these 'tennis stars,' as you call them?"

"From E-news. They're always having hissy fits when they don't get what they want. But what I'm failing to see is what you've done wrong. Why do you think they'd want to fire you?"

Miranda groaned, as she hugged her knees and rocked slightly.

"They were my suggestions, E. I suggested we change up her backhand and move her around the court differently. And then when Jase wasn't with us in Austin, I didn't manage to coach her through the tournament. She lost and she was totally pissed."

"Of course she was pissed—she lost! That doesn't mean it was your fault."

"They expected me to get her through and I dropped the ball. Not only that, we actually had a fight! I haven't had a fight with anyone since I was a kid. It felt horrible. I'm guessing Jase probably won't want me on the team now."

"Miranda, only Jodi can get Jodi through," Enid said patiently. "Your role is to support and advise, and yes, you're out of your depth given that you're only supposed to be assistant coach, but she still had access to Jason on the phone and so did you. Did he ever tell you that you were doing something wrong? Did he tell you to change what you were doing?"

Miranda shook her head. "No, but he was pretty preoccupied with the baby stuff."

"So, is it possible that maybe Jason dropped the ball?" Enid suggested gently.

"I don't know. I feel like I don't know anything at the moment." Miranda sighed deeply, and sat up straight. "Let's just talk about something else. What shall we make for dinner? What time did you say this Abby girl is coming round? I'm glad you've invited her, by the way. That's a very big step for you."

"I know!" Enid's eyes lit up. "She asked me what I was doing tonight. Apparently she wanted to take me to some new bar in Berkeley, but when I told her I was going to your place she was so sweet about it, I suddenly decided I should invite her to come along. You guys haven't really had a chance to hang out and it's probably about time you did."

"Well," Miranda teased, "I don't want to waste my precious time bonding with someone you're not going to keep around. How long has this one been on the scene? Four weeks? Five?"

"Actually, it's been two months. This weekend is our two month-a-versary." Enid's smirk was playful.

"Wow, congratulations. If I'd known, I would have gotten you a gift. Well, I'm glad. You know I like you to be sure before I hang out with your girlfriends; otherwise it just gets awkward."

"This is about as sure as I'm going to get," Enid said, lying back on the bed with a sigh. "She's actually quite dreamy. And sexy. God, she's so sexy." Enid gave a dramatic shiver. "She's got the most amazing body and when she kisses me I just get so—"

"Whoa," Miranda cut in, covering her ears with her hands. "I get the picture! She's hot, you like her; she's coming for dinner. It's all good news."

Enid laughed and threw a pillow at her friend.

"Careful," Miranda warned with artificial seriousness as she caught the pillow. "You could knock me out the window."

"That was the idea!"

"Hey! Watch it or I won't make nice with your girlfriend at dinner. Now, speaking of dinner, what are we going to make? We need a plan."

Miranda's phone suddenly broke into the opening bars of "Footloose," and she grinned self-consciously at Enid who looked askance.

"What? I like it," Miranda said sheepishly. "It makes me happy." She hopped off the window seat and grabbed her phone from the dresser.

"Shit, it's Jodi," she said, brandishing the phone at Enid.

"Answer it," Enid encouraged.

Miranda stared at the phone for another second, her face screwed up in uncertainty.

"Miranda! Answer it!" Enid hissed, throwing another pillow at her.

"Okay! Okay!" Miranda turned slightly away, and punched the "call accept" button.

"Jodi, hi," she said into the phone, frowning at Enid. Enid stuck out her tongue.

"Hi, sorry to bother you on your day off." Jodi's voice sounded official and distant down the line. Miranda felt a flutter of nervousness course through her abdomen.

"It's no problem, what can I do for you?"

"Jase and I have discussed it and we've agreed that it's best for him and Sal if he doesn't come with us to Vancouver next week. Sal's definitely on the mend but she's not quite over the infection and it's better for him to be close to home until the doctors give her the all clear."

"Okay," Miranda said with concern, wondering where the conversation was going.

"The thing is—" Jodi sounded hesitant. "Jase is written down on my visa for Canada as my coach and I need to get it changed to your name. We can rush it through in time but I need your signature on the paperwork tonight in order to get it done before we leave. I was wondering if I could come and find you and get you to sign the form?"

"Sure, of course!" Miranda answered, a wave of relief rushing through her. This definitely didn't sound like she was being fired. "I'm just at home. I'd come to you, but I've got friends coming for dinner. Would you mind coming out here?"

"No problem. I can come to you," Jodi answered quickly. "I'm sorry to bust in on your night but I'll just swing in and out. Jase was going to do it, but I told him to stay with Sal. I can get all this worked out if you can sign it tonight."

"Yes, of course. I'll give you my address. Do you have a car?" Miranda asked, suddenly curious. She had only ever seen Jodi take cabs or be driven by others.

"I've got Jase and Sal's other car. I already have your address from the visa application so I can be with you by six if that's okay?"

Miranda agreed and they rung off. She stood in the middle of the room staring at the phone in surprise.

"Jodi's coming over," she said to Enid.

"I got that," Enid said dryly. "But why?"

"She needs me to sign some form so she can change our visas for Canada."

"So, you're not fired then," Enid smirked.

"I guess not," Miranda replied, looking sheepish. "She said she'll be here around six. Hey, when's Abby coming?"

"Also around six. Shall we invite Jodi to stay for dinner?"

"Oh no, I don't think so. She sounded very businesslike. And she's in a rush. She said she's just going to run in and get the form signed."

Jodi sat next to Miranda, who frowned in concentration, studying the forms before her.

"So I just need to fill out this bit, right?" Miranda asked, her clear blue eyes looking up to meet Jodi's.

"That's right, just the occupation and address stuff."

Miranda bent over the form, tucking her hair behind her ear as she wrote in her details. Jodi admired Miranda's slim fingers and the strong line of her slender wrist. She has really beautiful hands, she thought. She remembered briefly the feel of Miranda's hand in hers at the USTA party. Heat ran through her as she thought of taking Miranda's hand in her own again.

"Would you like a glass of wine, Jodi?" Enid held up the bottle from behind the kitchen bench where she was busily preparing and chopping vegetable tidbits. "We're having white but we've got red, if you prefer." Jodi took in the proffered bottle, oblivious to the glare Miranda shot at her friend.

The kitchen was cool and pretty. A welcome light breeze floated in from the garden; the hanging plaits of garlic by the window swung gently. Jodi suddenly wished she could stay here and join in, to revel in the relaxed, friendly atmosphere. It had been ages since she'd simply hung out with friends on a Saturday night, making dinner and laughing together.

Reluctantly, she refused. "Thanks, but I don't want to take up your time. I'm sorry to be busting in on you like this anyway."

"Hey, it's fine," Enid reassured her. "You're not busting in, is she Miranda? Have a glass. This one is cheap," she continued, as she pretended to study the bottle, "with slight overtones of nasty. But it's cold and it goes down easy. Doesn't it, Miranda," Enid said again, pointedly prompting her friend.

"Of course, you're not taking up our time!" Miranda quickly joined in. "The wine is suitably bad but please do have a glass. You might as well, while we're sorting out these forms."

"Ok, well if you're sure you don't mind. That'd be great, thanks," Jodi said impulsively. The mood in the kitchen was cheerful and she didn't really feel like heading home alone to her hotel. She had lost contact with a lot of her friends when she and Tara had moved out to the lake, devoting herself instead to their relationship. It had been hard reconnecting with friends when it had all come tumbling down. Some friends were still mad with her for retreating, some had moved away, some had moved on with their own lives. She had tried to explain her situation to those she had reached out to—she'd never had a serious relationship before, and she had become lost without tennis to ground and direct her. Tara had seemed like the island to her storm, the rock that anchored her in the ocean of confusion. Some friends had been more forgiving than others, and Jodi had learnt a serious lesson about friendships. They needed effort and attention. Like houseplants, really. Something she also didn't have too many of, what with living in the hotel. For a moment, Jodi was struck by the near emptiness of her life. *I need to get out more, and I need to find a place to live. After the wildcard*, she resolved.

Enid presented Jodi with a glass of wine and she took a sip, giving a tiny shudder as the sharp, tangy wine prickled her taste buds.

"Told you." Enid said, grinning impishly at her. "It's not the best, but after a couple of glasses you'll hardly notice that aftertaste."

"It's fine," Jodi lied, taking another small sip. Again, the sharpness of the wine struck her, causing a little shiver.

"Really?" Enid cocked her head quizzically.

Jodi laughed. "Okay, it is kind of awful but strangely, I'm enjoying it." She gazed around the kitchen, taking in the posies of dried wildflowers and Tibetan prayer flags fluttering over the garden window. "This is a beautiful room."

"Thanks," Enid replied. "I like to think I had a hand in making it so."

Miranda snorted and Jodi caught something that sounded like a muttered, "I bet you do."

"Miranda's had this place for years. Her aunty willed it to her when we were nineteen, but she really needed my designer's touch to bring it all together." Enid glanced around the room with satisfaction.

"You painted the room, E," Miranda said dryly, not looking up from the paperwork. "I'm not sure that counts as bringing it all together."

"And I chose the colors," Enid pouted. "Without me you would have chosen some kind of hideous green or something. I really saved her from a terrible interior faux pas," she said conspiratorially to Jodi.

If Miranda had had this place since she was nineteen, Jodi calculated, Enid and Miranda must have lived there together for almost ten years! They seemed so easy and happy, and with a pang she realized she wanted to know that feeling for herself.

"I think that's done." Miranda put down the pen and slid the forms over to Jodi. "Can you check and see I've done it right?"

"Sure." Jodi ran her eyes over the papers, shuffling through the pages to check that each section was correct. "Looks good to me. Oh, no wait, here, you've missed this bit."

"Where?" Miranda leaned over, scrutinizing the part of the page where Jodi was pointing. Their knees slid against each other under the table, and Jodi could feel the warmth of Miranda's bare leg against her own. Jodi's pulse quickened and she fought the urge to lean in closer and put her hand down to rest on Miranda's strong, shapely thigh.

"Oh right, I see, sorry. I did miss that." Miranda took the papers back and Jodi instantly missed the touch where her leg had been.

The chime of the doorbell startled Jodi. She looked up and caught Enid watching her. She hoped her tan would hide her blush. *What am I thinking?* She gave herself a mental shake. Lusting after Enid's girlfriend in front of her definitely counted as poor form.

"That'll be Abby," Enid called, heading through the quaint archway that separated the kitchen from the foyer and the front door.

Enid was back a second later dragging a self-conscious-looking, pretty brunette by the hand.

"Miranda," Enid cried sternly. "Snap your head out of those papers and say hi to Abby."

Miranda looked up with a quick smile for the newcomer.

"Hi Abby," Miranda said warmly, getting up from the table to give Abby a welcoming hug.

"Abby this is Jodi, the tennis player I've been working for," Miranda said, turning to the table to make introductions. "Jodi, meet Abby, Enid's girlfriend."

"Hi." Jodi jumped up to shake hands, confusion momentarily showing on her face. "Enid's girlfriend?"

"Yes," Enid said slowly, a sudden look of wariness crossing her face. "Why?"

"Oh well, I thought, I mean…" Jodi trailed off awkwardly, looking from one face to another as she fought her bewilderment.

A look of understanding flashed over Enid's face and she broke out in a wide grin. "You thought Miranda and I were together?" she crowed.

"Er, yes, well, I guess I did," Jodi stammered.

"Oh God." Miranda pretended to shudder. "Not even on a desert island, hey, E?" She elbowed her friend jokingly in the ribs.

"Not if you were the last woman on earth," Enid rejoined, laughing uproariously. "This woman, on the other hand," she said, slipping her hand around Abby's waist, "this woman is definitely my girlfriend. Now, who wants another drink? Jodi, have you finished that horrible wine? We've got another bottle that's even worse already chilling in the fridge. And what can I get you, babe?" she asked, giving Abby a squeeze.

"I'll have a beer, thanks," Abby replied, with an adoring look at Enid.

"Coming right up."

"Hey, what about me?" Miranda asked, sounding injured.

"You'll have to get your own drinks from now on, Miranda. We don't want anyone getting the wrong idea." Enid smirked. "Jodi? You brave enough to try the other bottle?"

"I should go and let you guys get on with your dinner," Jodi replied stoically. She really didn't want to leave. "I've taken up enough of your time already."

"Why don't you stay for dinner," Miranda suggested, lightly touching her arm. "Enid's made enough food for the whole neighborhood and we could use your help getting through it."

"Oh yes, Jodi," Enid chimed in. "You should stay. We've got tons of food and it's better to be even numbers. Also, Abby's been telling me she wants to know more about tennis and I didn't want Miranda to be the one to tell her in case she gets it wrong, you know?"

"Hey!" Miranda protested, laughing.

"Oh well, we can't have that," Jodi replied, smiling affectionately at Miranda. She definitely wanted to stay. She wanted to share in this beautiful evening with these bright and entertaining women. "I think I'm right for wine at the moment but I'd love to stay, thank you."

"Great." Miranda gathered up the paperwork and passed it over to Jodi. "I think this is all done. Want to help me bring some plates out to the garden? I think we'll eat outside tonight."

The last light of dusk was failing as Jodi sat back in her chair and placed her hands over her stomach.

"I am absolutely stuffed," she declared with a happy sigh. "That was the best lasagna I think I've ever had. My compliments to the chefs."

"I'll second that," Abby added. "It was restaurant quality."

"Aw shucks, guys." Enid tried to look modest. "Thanks. We haven't done a big cook-up like that for ages, have we Mirry?"

Jodi noted the nickname, enjoying the familiarity between the two friends.

"That we haven't," Miranda replied

"And you grew most of the salad veggies?" Abby asked Miranda. "I don't seem to have any luck with my garden. The only things I can grow are weeds."

"Ah, well, you need an herb garden, then," Miranda replied, laying her knife and fork in the center of her plate. She leant across the table and lit the candles on an old, rusted candelabra. "Herbs will flourish in your garden like weeds, and you can eat them, so they're the best of both worlds, really."

The flickering candles cast a warm glow, accenting the approaching darkness. Jodi took a deep breath, inhaling the warm garden smells as she tipped her head back and looked up at the sky. The first stars were gradually making themselves known in the blue-black expanse and she felt her heart jolt in her chest. I'm happy, she thought, as she allowed the tiny thrill inside her to grow. Abby had her arm loosely draped around Enid's petite shoulder, the couple sat close together now that dinner was over. Jodi glanced at Miranda and quickly looked away, startled to find Miranda watching her. *I want to hold Miranda like that,* Jodi thought, her heart skipping a beat. *I want her to be closer.* Jodi's mind seemed to empty as the thudding of her heart took over. Risking another glance, the cornflower blue eyes were still on her and this time she met them steadily.

The falling night seemed to give them a moment of privacy and Jodi studied Miranda's impenetrable gaze from under her lashes. She wondered if Miranda could possibly know the sudden electric desire that pulsed through her as she lowered her eyes to stare at the flames.

"So your next tournament is in Vancouver, Jodi?" Abby's voice cut across her thoughts.

"Uh, yes, that's right." Her own voice sounded far away. "We leave a week from Tuesday."

"And how's our Miranda working out as a coach?" Enid probed, her cheeky grin lit up by the candlelight. "Is she any good or would you prefer one of us to come with you?"

Miranda choked on her wine, spluttering as she admonished, "Enid!"

Jodi laughed, but just as quickly became serious as she regarded her assistant coach. "Actually Miranda's doing a very good job. She's got great ideas and endless passion for the game. And she doesn't seem to hold it against me for acting like a diva sometimes, so I'd say she's got the whole coach thing down pat, really." Jodi met Miranda's surprised look with a warm smile.

"Well, I've had plenty of practice with Enid, you see," Miranda replied with feigned modesty. "She's actually Sacramento's number one diva."

"Hey!" Enid cried. "Not in front of Abby, okay? She doesn't know that yet!"

Abby gave a warm chuckle, and leaned her head against Enid's. "Actually, babe, I did kind of suspect that. Only a true diva has rules about what can and can't be worn out to breakfast."

"Oh," Enid breathed, snuggling in closer. She tipped her head up to flutter her eyelids at her girlfriend. "And you're still here. You must really like me."

Abby's answer was a searing kiss, and Jodi and Miranda both laughed.

"Want to take the plates in with me?" Miranda touched Jodi's arm lightly. "This might be a good time to leave them to it."

"Sure thing."

They gathered up the mess of plates and cutlery, stacking serving spoons and salad bowls together. Jodi followed Miranda into the kitchen.

"I'll wash, you dry," Miranda directed, as she stationed herself behind the sink and threw a tea towel to Jodi. They fell into an easy rhythm, chatting comfortably together as they cleaned.

"So how long have Enid and Abby been together?" Jodi asked as she stacked another dry plate on the bench.

"Not that long really, about two months. But it's lining up to be the longest relationship Enid has had in forever, so it's kind of a big deal."

Peering out through the open window into the dark garden, Jodi could see the couple wrapped in each other's arms, Enid now perched on Abby's lap as they shared a private moment.

"They seem very happy together."

"I know. I'm so glad for them."

"What about you?" Jodi found herself asking, forcing a casual tone. She focused intently on the plate she was drying, not daring to look up.

"Me?"

"Do you have...I mean, are you... seeing anyone?"

"Me? No."

They fell silent, focusing on the task at hand.

"What about you?" Miranda asked abruptly, pausing as she held up a soapy plate. "How long have you and Lisa been seeing each other?"

"Me and Lisa?" Jodi's eyes widened in surprise. "Oh, no." She shook her head emphatically. "We're not together."

"What? But I thought..." Miranda trailed off.

"Nope. Jase asked me to speak with her about a publicity campaign and that's what we've been doing."

"But, what about Austin? She seemed, well, didn't she come to Austin just to see you?"

"Yeah," Jodi sighed, feeling awkward. She didn't really want to have to explain the whole kiss and misunderstanding to Miranda right now. "I think I may have given her the wrong impression."

"Gosh," Miranda giggled, "do you think?"

"Hey," Jodi swatted her with the tea towel. "Watch yourself. I'm still your boss you know."

Miranda grabbed the tea towel and held on, her eyes twinkling.

"Yes, but I'm your coach. I think you might need some advice in the dating department."

Jodi felt the spark between them flame in the naked air; the intensity of Miranda's gaze momentarily took her breath away. Miranda slowly pulled on the tea towel, drawing Jodi in closer to her, until they were standing inches apart.

"You're not with Lisa?" Miranda's eyes held the question, dark with emotion.

"I'm not," Jodi whispered.

As their lips met, Jodi melted easily into Miranda, arms wound lightly around her waist. Her lips were surprisingly soft and Jodi registered with shock the briefest touch of Miranda's tongue against her own. So this is what it feels like to kiss her, she thought distractedly. Alarm bells began to clang in her head and she sprang backwards, bumping against the pile of dishes she had dried.

"I- I can't do this," Jodi stammered, hugging her arms tightly to her chest as she pressed back against the bench. "I shouldn't—I can't." Under Miranda's intense gaze—her pupils wide and dark in her usually light blue eyes—Jodi felt desire and fear fight for first place inside of her. "I should go, I'm so sorry."

Jodi hurried to the table to retrieve her bag. She slipped it over her shoulder as she fled the room.

"Wait, Jodi!" Miranda's voice stopped her as she was pulling open the front door. Miranda brandished the wad of papers Jodi had brought for her. "Don't forget these."

Miranda's face was unreadable in the shadows of the doorway. Jodi took the papers and stuffed them quickly into her bag.

"Thank you. Please say goodbye to the others for me. I really should go."

Jodi lurched down the steps, then fumbled with the key as she let herself into the unfamiliar car. Her hands shook as she took off, her heart pounding out a tattoo in her ears. She revved the car unnecessarily, and peered through the darkness, driving too quickly down the suburban streets as she looked for a turn she recognized.

"Just pull over," she told herself. "Just pull over and get a grip."

Easing to a stop, she rooted around in her bag for her telephone, tapping open the GPS app when she found it. She typed in her hotel address with shaky fingers, and leaned back in her seat as the GPS processed her request.

"Shit," she cursed aloud. *What have I done?* The last thing she needed right now was any kind of complication. She couldn't deny the pull of attraction she felt for Miranda, with her wide, inviting smile and ocean blue eyes, but there could be no more kissing. Relationships, as she had learnt from Tara, were death to tennis, and she was trying her best right now to breathe life into a career that may have potentially been out cold for far too long to be revived. This was her only chance. Her last hurrah. If she didn't make it now she could hang up her racket forever. Oh, she would play the odd game with friends, maybe find a Saturday morning doubles team to join, but competitive, professional tennis would be over for her. Well, she was damned if she was going to jeopardize her chances now, having only just made the choice to put herself back out there again.

Jodi stared out into the night, oblivious to the phone in her hand as it displayed her route home. Her muscles burned from the constant training; her palms sported long, white blisters that would eventually turn themselves back into permanent callouses; her ego was battered and her pride was sore, but she was absolutely determined to keep going. She wanted to push her body to new limits, to see just how far she could go as an athlete. Would she get the wild card? Could she make it to the US Open? And if she did, how far could she go from there? Australia, Japan? The possibilities were endless. But there was no room in this picture for romance. Her schedule was punishing and she needed to focus. Distractions would derail her, and her relationship with Tara had shown her just how disastrously she could be derailed. Maybe later down the track, when she had taken her career as far as it could truly go, she could start to think about relationships again, but now was definitely not the time.

Jodi took a deep, unsteady breath, and tried to bring her mind to rest, a skill she had practiced many times on court. She placed the phone in the car cradle and pulled back out onto the road, following the directions of the computerized GPS voice.

It was a nice night and we got carried away, she told herself carefully. I'm sure Miranda will understand. Jodi concentrated on the road, and tried to dismiss the unmistakable ache inside of her.

I'm sure she'll understand.

CHAPTER THIRTEEN

Miranda jogged lightly from side to side on the baseline, poised to receive Jodi's serve. She adjusted her hat against the sun, and passed her sweatband across her forehead, mopping up the dampness. The ball hurtled towards her and she swung from the hip, driving the ball back across the net with precision. Jodi had set a punishing pace this morning and Miranda was stretched to her limits. The new drop shots were pushing her all over the court; Jodi seemed to have boundless energy, setting up the drill again and again.

"Ok, let's take a break," Jason called, waving them over to join him on the benches. "Nice work, Jodi, you're totally nailing the shot. I think we can move on to something else now. How you holding up, Miranda? You ok?"

Miranda nodded stoically. "Sure. What's next?" She twisted open a sports drink, gulping down the cool, sweet liquid. "Backhand? Footwork?"

Jodi put a foot up on the bench, stretching out her hamstrings. "I'd like to take it to the net for some volleys," she said. "Up for that Miranda?"

"Always," Miranda replied, capping her drink. She stood up quickly from the bench, trying not to let her weariness show. She rubbed the sweat from her neck and forehead, tossed her towel on the bench and followed Jodi back out to the court. She guessed they'd be done in another hour or so and thought longingly of a nice cool shower.

Set up, they began to volley, Miranda digging deep to keep the ball in play. Jodi's face was set in a firm line of concentration, her body arching and stretching as she placed her shots. Miranda was struck by the taut, graceful line of Jodi's body. They were close enough for Miranda to see the beads of sweat gathered on Jodi's skin, her tight shirt outlining the soft swell of her breasts straining against the thin material as she reached high for the ball. Miranda suddenly imagined herself with her hands on that shirt, lifting it over Jodi's head, pulling her in close to kiss the skin around her neck.

"Ouch!" Miranda rubbed her shoulder, massaging the spot where she had been struck full force by the ball.

"Oh gosh, sorry," Jodi called, running to the net. "Are you ok? I didn't mean to hit you, I thought you were ready for it!"

"Uh, yeah," Miranda mumbled, turning away to retrieve the ball. "I'm fine. I just lost concentration for a second."

Jodi looked at her watch. "We've been going for long enough this morning," she said, her face concerned. "Let's finish up for the day."

"I'm fine, really. I can keep going for as long as you want," Miranda reassured her.

"I think you've both had enough for today," Jason called across the court, scooping up balls with his racket and dropping them into the basket. "We don't want to overdo it. Why don't you guys hit the showers and we'll go grab some lunch."

Jodi stretched wearily and took off her cap. "Sounds like a plan," she said.

Miranda gratefully followed her off the court, embarrassed to have been caught out like that, but glad they were putting it down to tiredness.

"After lunch we'll settle our game plan for Vancouver," Jason said. "We've still got plenty of work to do off the court!"

Miranda was finding it hard to ignore the attraction she felt for Jodi; the memory of their kiss constantly catching her off guard. But Jason's increasing demands as they prepared for the tournament ahead left her little time or energy to dwell on it. Buckling down, she forced herself to ignore the distraction and embrace the grueling workload. By the time she and Jodi were on the plane, Miranda felt confident and re-focused on the task at hand, their kiss just a fading memory.

* * *

"The draw will be announced in twenty minutes, so please pick up your tournament packs and make yourselves familiar with the grounds," announced the handsome, boyish-looking official. He paused to look around at the group of coaches and tournament staff. Miranda felt a quick thrill as she observed some of the other coaches from previous tournaments and functions. *I can't believe I'm here*, she marveled.

"If you need transportation from your accommodation you must organize it with Shelley tonight." The official gestured to a red-haired woman seated behind a wide desk; she gave a small wave. "And otherwise, see me if there are any other issues. I'm Brett," he added, as he tapped his nametag, "and I'll be managing the logistics of your time here with us in Vancouver. Best of luck to you all."

As the group broke up, Miranda stuffed her hands in her pockets and headed over to the registration table to pick up Jodi's tournament pack. She knew a couple of people by name, and many by sight, and she could instantly tell that the caliber of this tournament was higher than any other she had attended.

"Richards," she said to the official behind the registration desk whose nametag read "Pamela." The woman shuffled through a large box of folders and pulled one out.

"Here you are, hon." She handed Miranda a folder with Jodi's name typed across its front. "All you'll need to know is in here. Consider it your tournament Bible," she said with a wide smile. "And have a great time."

"Thanks." Miranda took the folder. Her phone vibrated in her pocket.

Any news? The message read.

She smiled, and keyed in a reply. *You'll know as soon as we know, Jase, I promise.* Miranda could feel Jason's anxiety all the way up the coastline from California. She knew he was worried that Jodi would draw Jennifer Laurent in the first round of this tournament, but Miranda wasn't worried. She knew instinctively that Jodi could handle Laurent. Sure, their last match had been a disaster, but this time would be different. Miranda was resolved to do a much better job at coaching. She had spoken extensively with Jason about strategies to support Jodi and, as a team, they had worked diligently to position Jodi to beat technical players like Laurent. A tiny jolt shot through Miranda as she pictured Jodi running down the steps from her house after their kiss. She shook her head, determined not to think about that. A night of soul searching on the couch with Enid had straightened her out on that front.

"I wondered why she left in such a hurry," Enid had said, her tone uncharacteristically gentle when Miranda had finally spilled the beans about the kiss. Abby had gone to sleep in Miranda's spare room. They sat on the dark, back step, chatting comfortably.

"What do you think you want from this?" Enid asked.

"I don't know." Miranda sighed. "I'm so confused."

"What are you confused about?"

"All of it, I guess." She tipped her head back and stared at the bright wash of stars. "I don't really know if I kissed Jodi or if she kissed me, but I feel responsible and I guess it was probably inappropriate. I'm employed by the club as a coach—I'm not supposed to be fraternizing with the players. Anyway, her reaction made it pretty obvious how she feels."

"So then, why are you confused?"

"I don't know," Miranda said slowly, rubbing a hand over her eyes. "It was stupid. I don't want to jeopardize this job. It's a huge opportunity for me, as you know. I don't want to blow it, but I'd be lying if I said I wasn't attracted to her."

"She seemed keen enough." Miranda could hear the smirk in Enid's voice.

"It was a mistake, E. I shouldn't have done it. It was unprofessional. I don't know what came over me." Miranda felt momentarily breathless as she recalled Jodi, bumping against her playfully in the kitchen. Miranda had wanted to close the gap between them. *I wanted to kiss her. I still do.*

"I think I get what you're saying." Enid leaned forward and hugged her knees.

"You do?"

"Yeah. And I think you're right. This job is huge for you. You've waited a long time to figure out where you're going and what you're doing. You've always wanted to be involved with tennis and this job is pretty much a dream come true. I'd hate to see you lose that over some little crush."

"I don't have a crush," Miranda protested wearily.

"Okay, well, whatever it is, I think one day you'll be able to have both. An awesome career and a wonderful love life, but I don't know if Jodi is the right one for you. She's super focused on her career and your relationship isn't really set up for romance. She is your boss. Maybe this isn't the time to lose your head over a kiss."

"So, you think I should just forget about it?"

"Maybe. Is that what you think?"

"I guess so," Miranda replied heavily. "I really should concentrate on coaching and put this kind of stuff out of my mind."

"Hey," Enid put her arm around her friend. "It's going to be alright. You can be an old maid and come visit me and Abby in our beautiful home by the ocean. We'll have dinner parties and everyone will be excited to meet the famous tennis coach."

"Excellent. I can't wait." Miranda stretched wearily and stood up. "Bedtime now, I think."

* * *

"If you'll all gather 'round, we'll reveal the draw now." The announcement of Brett-the-official brought an immediate hush to the group. A bright, blank square on the projector screen awaited the first round of matches for this tournament. Brett clicked the mouse a few times and the screen came to life. As he adjusted the lens, a table of names bobbed into focus.

"Let me know if you have any questions about the draw. Otherwise, we'll see you all back here for your matches over the coming week."

Miranda located Jodi's name, halfway down the women's singles list and scribbled the unfamiliar opponent's name—A. Cutelle—in her notebook. She scanned the list for Laurent and noted that she was slated to play her first round match against Selena Kitchfield. *Laurent will slaughter her*, Miranda thought, noting down a few of the other matches in case Jodi or Jason asked her about them. Knowing that Jodi would be anxious to hear the results, she hurried to make their transportation arrangements and headed back to the hotel.

* * *

For dinner, Jodi and Miranda ate salads Miranda had picked up at a local organic store on her way back to the hotel, along with grilled salmon ordered up from the hotel kitchen. As usual, Jodi sprawled on the bed and Miranda perched on the desk with the laptop.

"Here." Miranda swiveled the laptop towards Jodi. "I've found some videos of Cutelle's matches and put them into a playlist. Want to watch them now?"

"Sure, fire away." Jodi shifted her plate onto the side table. "I'm stuffed."

Miranda set the laptop on the desk and settled next to Jodi on the bed. "Okay, the first one is a good example of her serve."

They scrutinized the moves of Jodi's soon-to-be opponent.

"She doesn't like the left side," Jodi remarked, as she watched Cutelle send a serve wide out of the court.

"I know, and watch how she hugs the baseline. This chick doesn't like to come forward."

"I don't know if I do either, anymore," Jodi said ruefully.

Miranda looked Jodi straight in the eye. "Jodi, you got spooked. You're fine at the net. In fact, you're more than fine. You're brilliant. You can own the whole court, and that's what makes you different. That's why you will win, because you're not afraid."

Jodi pursed her lips and reached for her drink.

"What if I do feel a bit afraid?"

Miranda paused and took a deep breath. She needed to get this moment right. "Well, it's okay to be a little bit afraid, I guess. It's pretty normal when you're faced with a daunting task. But once you've realized you're afraid, you need to turn the fear into excitement and anticipation. You love to play tennis. And you're a natural. So, you need to go out there and *love* what you do. Have a riot."

Jodi grinned. "I do love it."

"Yeah, you do."

Jodi sipped her drink and returned her attention to the video. She gently elbowed Miranda.

"Thanks, coach."

Miranda suppressed a smile and got up from the bed. "Shall we watch the next one?"

* * *

The morning's match ended quickly. Jodi powered through Cutelle as if she meant to take no prisoners. Miranda sat in the bleachers, smirking, her cap pulled low to block out the already beating hot sun. Clearly, Jodi had clearly taken her pep talk to heart.

In the locker room, Miranda was elated. "You looked like you enjoyed that!" Miranda exclaimed, placing a drink next to Jodi as Jodi unlaced her shoes.

"Actually, I did," Jodi replied. "I finally got over myself and had some fun." Her eyes sparkled with excitement.

"You were awesome. Jase will be sorry he missed that but I managed to get a bit of the match on video so we can send him some highlights."

"He'll love that." Jodi kicked off her shoes and grabbed her towel. "I'm disgustingly sweaty. I hate to think how hot it's going to be out there by the afternoon. I'm going to grab a shower and we can get out of here."

* * *

That night, with Jason on speakerphone, they filled him in on the day's events and Jodi's next opponent.

"Kitchfield lost to Laurent," Jodi told him. "I've got O'Reilly tomorrow. I remember her from that weird tournament in Dallas, like, forever ago."

"Oh yeah, she's no match for you. I can't believe she's still hanging around." Jason's voice got serious. "Now go get your beauty sleep and call me tomorrow. I predict you will wipe up the court with her."

Jodi and Miranda both laughed and promised to call him after the match.

Jason's prediction turned out to be accurate. The next day, Jodi settled the match quickly in two straight sets: 6-0, 6-0.

Miranda enjoyed the confidence and ease with which Jodi played, covering the court from top to bottom without hesitation. The tournament buzzed about Jodi and the press asked for interviews.

"Make them wait until after the semi-finals," Jason had counseled. "Publicity is good but you both need to concentrate right now. Jodi doesn't need the press poking and prodding her. She can give them a quick interview before the finals."

"That's if I make it to the finals!"

"The finals have your name written all over them, Jodes."

Jodi's winning streak stretched through the week, but by Friday night she was holed up in her room with an icepack on her neck.

"Don't worry," Miranda coached. "Worrying always makes things worse. If you worry, you'll get all tight and sore. Just relax and breathe through it. The physical therapist says you'll be fine by tomorrow. Your neck is just a little strained."

"What if it's not?"

"If it's not, you'll play with a slightly sore neck," Miranda answered. "I'm sure you've played with worse injuries, no?"

Jodi nodded ruefully. "I have. I once played a whole match with a broken bone in my foot."

"Okay! Well, there you go. I'm not sure that's something you'd want to repeat, but I guess you get where I'm coming from. But really," Miranda emphasized, "you're going to be fine for tomorrow."

"I really want to win this." Jodi's voice was low and intense as she studied her hands.

"I know you do, Jodi. And I don't see any reason why you won't."

"It's Laurent. She's playing incredibly well."

"And so are you. And you're smarter and more experienced. She's only been on the circuit for a couple of years. I've got no doubt she's going to be a formidable force in the future, but she's really not someone for you to worry about right now. Let's not lose our heads, okay?"

Jodi nodded and shifted uncomfortably on the bed. Moving the strap of her singlet, she flicked her long hair out of the way and adjusted the ice pack on her neck.

"Hey, you want me to rub some more of that salve onto your neck before you hit the sack?" Miranda asked.

"That'd be great, thanks."

Grabbing the tube of salve from the bathroom, Miranda stood next to the bed where Jodi sat, and placed her hands lightly on Jodi's bare shoulders.

"Now, just relax and try to let go of all your stress," she said.

The salve felt cool compared to the heat radiating from Jodi's skin. Miranda pressed her thumbs gently into the tense muscles, remembering the massage techniques she had learned from a sports health course.

"Oh God," Jodi groaned and leaned back slightly. "That feels amazing."

"Pressure's okay?"

"Oh, yes. It's perfect," she purred.

"Good, I'm glad."

The velvety softness of Jodi's neck left Miranda a little breathless. As Jodi leaned back a bit more and rested against Miranda's belly, the heat of their connection filled Miranda with desire. She wanted to wrap her arms around Jodi and kiss her, but instead withdrew her hands. She gave Jodi a little pat on the shoulder.

"That should do it," Miranda said primly.

"Oh, thanks." Jodi seemed surprised by Miranda's abruptness. She swiveled around. "That was really nice."

"No problem. Now," Miranda cleared her throat, "get some rest and I'll see you in the morning."

"Alright." Jodi stretched out on the bed. "Hope you sleep well, too."

Miranda paused at the door. "You're going to nail it tomorrow, Jodi," she said. "This tournament is yours."

"I sure hope so."

Early the next morning, Jodi found Miranda at breakfast in the hotel dining room.

"No pain," Jodi grinned.

"Excellent!" Miranda exclaimed.

They ate what Miranda had coined a "finals breakfast," consisting of eggs, a coffee for Miranda, and a protein shake for Jodi. It was enough to fuel her through her big match without making her feel heavy.

As she sat in the bleachers later that morning, Miranda was glad they had eaten well. The heat was punishing, and while Jodi's hard-won experience clearly gave her an advantage over the younger Laurent, she needed every ounce of her energy. Jodi widened the score gap with every point, drawing out their rallies with nail-biting intensity. Laurent was precise and seemingly unruffled, but Jodi continuously forced her out of her comfort zone. Miranda was transfixed.

After winning the first set, Jodi increased her pressure on the young player, sending her around the court in a complicated dance that had the desired effect; Laurent tired and Jodi won the match with quiet confidence.

Miranda cheered along with the rest of the crowd, filled with pride as Jodi accepted the tournament trophy and victoriously held it up to the crowd. *Thank God*, she thought, as the tension of the day finally left her. *What a mission*. It was exhausting just to watch. She knew Jodi would be tired, but the high from the win would easily carry her through the night. Ducking out of her seat as Jodi finished a short speech of thanks, Miranda trotted up the steps and out of the stadium to the player's locker room. She wanted to be there when Jodi arrived.

Jodi hugged Miranda when she saw her in the locker room, a gesture that surprised even her. Despite the small group of tournament officials and friends who gathered to congratulate her, Jodi wanted a moment alone with Miranda.

"You did it!" Miranda gave her a quick squeeze then held up her cell phone. "Video call," she said, handing over the phone.

Jason sported a wide grin as he gave Jodi a thumbs up, congratulating her warmly. "Wait, Sal's here too. Jump in, honey." Sal's face appeared next to Jason's.

"We're so proud of you, Jodi."

"Thanks, you guys. I couldn't have done it without you," Jodi replied with a wide smile.

"Call me for a proper debriefing tomorrow," Jason requested. "I want to hear all about it. Now you can go do those interviews, okay?"

"Will do, coach."

Jodi felt dazed as she looked around. She recognized some of the tournament officials, members of the press, and even some other players.

The tournament director rushed up and shook her hand. "We're glad to have you back in the game, Jodi," he said.

Jodi took his hand warmly and wracked her brain for his name. "And I'm glad to be here." Jodi looked for Miranda, who had stepped aside. "This is my coach, Miranda."

"Nice to meet you Miranda." The man looked confused. "I'm Bernie Couch. Jason Stovack no longer around?"

"I'm really just her assistant coach," Miranda responded quickly. "Jason and his wife are having a baby, and he had to stay home to deal with some medical stuff. He'll be back on board next week, we hope."

"Ah," the director smiled. "He's a good man to have in your corner, Jodi."

"Absolutely," Jodi nodded.

"We have a winner's conference lined up for you in an hour in the main hub. Let us know if you need anything else."

"I need to shower. My shirt is starting to become one with my skin."

The director laughed good-naturedly. "Well then, you must do that. I'll take care of these guys," he gestured to the group.

Jodi grabbed a towel from her bag and slipped into a cubicle.

"Ladies and gentleman," the director announced, "Ms. Richards is going to need half an hour. I suggest we give her some time to clean up and catch her breath before the press conference."

The small group murmured its approval and cleared out, leaving Miranda and the tournament director alone in the locker room.

"She's doing extremely well." he commented. "How long have you been on the team?"

"About a month and a half. It's gone by so quickly it only feels like a few days, really!"

"And she's competing for the wildcard?" he asked.

Miranda stalled. Jodi didn't like people to know her business and Miranda wasn't really sure if she was supposed to talk about this kind of thing publicly. She recalled their conversation at the California USTA tennis dinner. Jason's voice echoed in her head. *We need to let these USTA people know that she's here and she's in the market for the US Open wildcard.*

"Yeah," Miranda said. "That's the idea."

"Well, at this rate, I think she'll get it." He slapped her on the shoulder. "We'll see you at the press conference in an hour."

With the press conference finally over, a tournament steward ushered a tired Jodi and Miranda through a maze of bleak grey service corridors, running under the tennis center towards the building's back exit.

"We've got a car waiting for you out here," he said as they followed behind him. "Most of the crowds have cleared out by now but this will help you leave quickly in case there are still some fans lurking around."

"I don't know how you ever find your way around here!" Miranda exclaimed, "It's a total rabbit warren."

"You get used to it," the steward said, "once you've done it a few hundred times you hardly ever get lost. So here we are." He opened a nondescript door with a glowing green exit sign above it, and bright sunlight streamed into the corridor. Both women shielded their eyes as they looked out. They appeared to be at some kind of loading dock. A couple of workers in dusty blue overalls were stacking boxes of what looked like juice onto a trolley, and they nodded in greeting as Jodi and Miranda stepped out of the building. A silver car was parked by the entrance to the dock and two men stood leaning easily against the car.

"That's your driver," the steward said, "but I'm not sure who the other man is."

Jodi took a step forward, squinting against the afternoon glare. *Could it be?* It had to have been over two years since she'd last seen him, but it was hard to mistake the tall, lanky figure with the slightly hunched shoulders.

"It's my dad," she said quietly.

"Oh, right! Cool!" the steward seemed relieved. "Even though we use this exit we sometimes still get crazy stalker fans who sneak around back here. Ok if I leave you to it now?"

"Yes, thank you," Jodi shook his hand distractedly and jogged over to the car to greet her father. Mystified, Miranda followed behind. Jodi had never mentioned her father. Knowing that Jodi and her sister had grown up with their Nan, Miranda had assumed Jodi's parents weren't alive.

The driver greeted Miranda, taking the racket bags from her.

"I hope this ok," he murmured. "He said he was her dad and all."

"Yeah, I think it is," Miranda said, feeling puzzled as she watched Jodi give her father a quick kiss.

"Well, you girls let me know if you need me. I'll wait in the car."

"Miranda." Jodi called her over, "This is my father, David. Dad, meet my coach, Miranda Ciccone."

Jodi's father gripped Miranda's hand awkwardly. "Nice to meet you Miranda, you're obviously doing great work with my daughter."

"Thank you, sir," Miranda said, as he gave her hand one last pump and dropped it quickly. "I do what I can but she's doing all the hard work."

"What are you doing here, Dad?" Jodi's tone was light, but Miranda could sense a tightness behind the words. She placed a protective hand on Jodi's shoulder.

"I had a conference in Vancouver this week. One of my associates was talking up the tournament and how there was this star player we all just had to watch. Imagine my surprise when I realised it was you he was talking about! So I came to see you play. You were really something out there."

"Well, it's nice to see you, Dad. But you should have called and let me know you were here. How did you even find me back here anyway?"

"Oh, I just spoke to one of the stewards and told him I was your dad. He let me know I could wait for you out here."

Miranda made a mental note to email the tournament director about their security arrangements. There wasn't much point in having a secure back entrance if the staff let any old person know where it was.

"That's great, Dad," Jodi seemed tired. "I'll be sure to tell Ally we bumped into you."

"Would you—could I—" her dad stumbled over the words, "perhaps I could take you out for dinner tonight? Miranda, you'd be welcome to join us."

"You should have called," Jodi repeated, avoiding his eyes. "I've—I've already got plans for tonight."

"Of course." His face fell. "I did think that might be the case. No matter."

"Look, why don't I call you when I get back to Sacramento?" she suggested, her face softer. "We can catch up next time you're in town. I'll tell Ally too. The three of us can go out to dinner."

"I'd like that," her father replied, his face brightening. He straightened up and moved away from the car. "I'd best leave you to it. Nice to meet you, Miranda."

"And you, sir," Miranda replied, letting her hand finally drop from Jodi's shoulder. "Safe travels."

Jodi's father stooped, pulling Jodi into a brief hug. "Bye Jodi."

"Bye Dad."

Jodi stepped away from her father and opened the car door, sliding across the back seat to make room for Miranda. Miranda scooted in after her and the driver started the car.

"Ready to go ladies?" he asked, watching them from his rear-view mirror.

"Yes, please," Jodi replied.

Their car swept past Jodi's father and he raised his hand in a wave. *He looks lonely*, Miranda thought, as they drove on. Jodi did not turn around to catch another glimpse of him. She stared straight ahead, her jaw clenched tightly as they left the tennis centre.

"You ok?" Miranda asked, reaching over to rub Jodi's arm.

Not turning her head, Jodi gave a nod. She took Miranda's hand and held it tightly in her own. Miranda gave her hand a squeeze.

"Bit of a shock for you?" she asked, gently.

Jodi nodded again, and turned to meet Miranda's gaze. Her dark eyes were bright with the sheen of unshed tears. "You could say that," she said, with a slight smile.

They continued to hold hands, Miranda rubbing her thumb gently over Jodi's as the car took them through the busy streets of downtown Vancouver, towards their hotel.

"Do you really have plans tonight?" Miranda asked, quietly.

"Sort of. We could go to the tournament party at Retro

Club. I've heard it's a really cool bar." Jodi paused. "I don't really care what we do, I just want to celebrate tonight."

"And dinner with your dad doesn't fall into that basket?"

"Definitely not." Jodi gave a hollow laugh. "I haven't seen him for years. We barely speak. He's not a bad man or anything, but he's just never really been there for us and I don't feel close to him in any way. Seeing him just stirs up sad old memories."

Miranda squeezed Jodi's hand lightly. "I think I get what you mean."

"Ally and I grew up with our Nan," Jodi said, looking out the window as she spoke. "Our mum died when I was really young and Dad just faded out of the picture. He couldn't deal with us, I guess. I don't blame him, but I don't really know him. He used to send letters and stuff—now he texts or emails occasionally." Jodi smiled ruefully, turning to face Miranda. "Not even for birthdays, just when he remembers, I suppose."

Miranda's heart ached for the vulnerable child Jodi had been. She thought she could still see a glimpse of that child now. Instinctively she raised Jodi's hand to her lips and kissed it lightly. Jodi let go of Miranda's hand and unbuckled her seatbelt, sliding across the leather seats to sit next to her. She re-buckled her seat belt and slipped her hand back into Miranda's, leaning her head against Miranda's shoulder. Her body pressed warmly against Miranda's arm and Miranda felt her pulse quicken.

"I'm sorry you've had a hard time," Miranda murmured, intoxicated by the delicate smell of Jodi's perfume. Impulsively she dropped a soft kiss on Jodi's glossy head. Jodi snuggled in closer, holding Miranda's hand more tightly.

"It feels ok now."

They stayed pressed closely together for the rest of the drive, watching the streets go past until the driver pulled up at their hotel. Reluctantly, Miranda straightened up, letting go of Jodi's hand.

"Well, let's make sure we really celebrate tonight then, hey?" she said, smiling into Jodi's eyes.

"I'd like that," Jodi replied. "Thanks for being a good friend, Miranda."

Miranda climbed out of the car, grabbing Jodi's racket bags from the driver and thanking him. *Good friend, huh*, she thought, as they walked into the hotel. Her pulse was still knocking about erratically as they stood at the counter to check in. She shoved her hands in her pockets, resisting the urge to wrap an arm around Jodi's waist and pull her back in close. *I can be a good friend.*

CHAPTER FOURTEEN

"So, who are these people again?" Miranda leaned over the edge of the ferry and stared at little frothy waves produced by the weight of the massive ship as it cut through the bright, blue ocean.

"Karen and Mark," Jodi replied. "Karen and I went to high school together and they're two of the sweetest people you'll ever meet. Now please, don't lean so far over the edge." Her heart jumped as Miranda tipped herself a little further over the rail, and then shot her a cheeky grin. "People *do* fall off you know," Jodi admonished, "and they won't stop the boat for you. I'll just have to go to dinner without you."

Miranda laughed and hauled herself back over the rail. "Well, we can't have that, now can we? I wouldn't get to meet the sweetest people on the planet, and I wouldn't get to go to Vancouver Island, which sounds terribly romantic. Will anyone else be there?"

Jodi chuckled. "I actually don't know. Probably. They love to entertain, so it wouldn't surprise me if they made it a bit of a night."

"I can't believe we're doing this!" Miranda's smile was infectious. "I'm so glad your friends invited us to dinner. I never imagined we'd have time to do something so super cool."

"Well, you did say you wanted to do some touristy things. Actually, this is pretty rare for me, too. Usually Jase rushes me out of the city as soon as the tournament is over, but for some reason this time he gave us an extra day. Maybe the flights were cheaper tomorrow."

Miranda hung onto the railing and shook her hair as the wind picked up. Jodi wished she had a camera to capture the moment: Miranda's tousled blonde hair, and eyes that matched the sparkle of the water. It was a stunning, clear afternoon and Miranda seemed joyful. Jodi's own hair was tied up firmly and she was enjoying the cool breeze on her neck.

The edge of the mainland receded quickly as the ferry powered across the Strait of Georgia. In front of them, the afternoon was a wash of blues; the sky met the ocean in an almost seamless horizon.

"Well, I don't really care what the reason is," Miranda said. "I, for one, am going to make the most of it. How long is this ride?"

"About an hour and a half."

"And they're picking us up on the other side?"

"Yep, that's the plan."

"And we're staying the night. That'll be fun. Better than staying in the hotel again. I feel claustrophobic in there."

"You definitely won't have that problem at Karen and Mark's," Jodi said with a knowing smile.

An hour later, they bumped their way across the island in Karen's rusty little car. Jodi sat in the front while Miranda stretched out in the back.

"Hey," Miranda muttered.

Jodi looked back. "What's wrong?" she asked, puzzled by Miranda's confused look.

"I didn't realize it would be so huge! You said we were coming to an island but this is like a whole new country."

Karen howled with laughter as she turned down a small, tree-lined street. Glimpses of the ocean flickered through the trees. "You're right there," she said in a slow Californian drawl. "Vancouver Island is small in Canadian terms, but it's bigger than some European and African countries. It's a shame you're not staying longer. There's so much incredible beauty to experience here."

"Luckily, we're going to your house," Jodi chimed in. "She'll get a small taste of that beauty there."

Karen sighed happily and turned onto a long, gravel driveway. "I hope you like nice views, Miranda," she said.

From the back seat, Miranda gasped; even Jodi—who had seen this view many times before—was struck by the sight before them. Set on the edge of a craggy, black cliff was a small brick house, tiny against the vast expanse of ocean and dark rock face.

Karen turned off the engine. Jodi felt her spirits lift as the three women sat for a moment in silence.

"Home sweet home," Karen said eventually. She threw off her seat belt and jumped out of the car. "Come on, Mark's excited to see you."

Jodi and Miranda hauled their bags from the car and trotted after their host.

"Jodi!" Mark cried, clattering down the stone steps to embrace her. "You should stay longer," he chided with good humor.

"Hey, I just got here!" Jodi laughed. "Give me a break! Mark, this is Miranda, one of my coaches."

Mark grabbed Miranda's hand and pumped it warmly. "Great to meet you. You're obviously doing wonders with Jodi. She seems almost human."

"Hey!" Jodi laughed as they started for the house. "Take my rackets, would you? They're heavy."

"Ah now, see?" He raised his eyes pointedly at Miranda. "That's the Jodi we know and love."

"Oh, yes." Miranda teased. "She makes me shine her shoes every day and peel her a grape in the evenings before bed."

Mark barked with laughter and threw his heavy arm around Miranda's shoulder. "I'm glad she brought you."

Jodi settled into a warm glow as she carefully edged in through the small door. She heard Miranda's sharp breath behind her as they stepped into the enormous living room where wall-to-wall windows overlooked the ocean. From where they stood the grass outside seemed to run away to nowhere, the steep cliff face out of sight, leaving a feeling of being able to step out of the back door and into the rippling blue.

"I see you don't have much to look at," Miranda said dryly.

Karen and Mark both chuckled, accustomed to the arresting effect their house had on others.

"It's a small house," Karen gestured to the space around them. "We don't have hundreds of rooms, but what we saved on real estate we spent on a seascape."

Jodi kicked off her shoes. It felt good to be back in her friend's beautiful home. She had visited a few times over the years and felt at ease here. She and Karen kept in touch by email, mostly birthday phone calls and around other important occasions. She gazed out the window and remembered the terribly uncomfortable visit she had had here with Tara, early on in their relationship.

Tara had, of course, been enraptured by the ocean panorama and had inquired obsessively about the value of the property. Oblivious to Karen and Mark's disinterest in selling, she urged them to have the place appraised. When Tara became pushy, Jodi had felt more and more embarrassed, hardly able to meet her friends' eyes when she hugged them goodbye. They had never really spoken of it, but Karen had been warmly supportive when Jodi emailed her about the break-up.

Jodi shook off the memories. "Here, give me your bag," she said to Miranda. "I'll toss our stuff in the spare room."

"I'll come with you. I'd like to see it."

Jodi padded down the cool, wooden hallway and opened the second door.   "That's their bedroom." She pointed to the door across the hallway. "The bathroom is over there."

The room was sparsely furnished, but the same breathtaking vista was visible through a window smaller than the one in the living room. A large inflatable mattress sat next to the window, and the fold-out couch had been turned into a second bed.

"Which do you prefer?" Jodi asked politely. "Blow-up or fold-out?"

Miranda dropped her bag and jumped onto the blow-up bed, which bobbed up and down beneath her. "I'd like this bed next to the window if you don't mind. I can watch the stars and the ocean all night."

"Be my guest." Jodi stretched out on the sofa bed. "I'll have the same view from the couch and I find them infinitely preferable to blow-ups."

Karen popped her head in the door. "Would you ladies like a drink before dinner? Mark's got the bar going if you'd like to join us."

"Sounds good to me." Jodi groaned as she rolled off the bed. "Every muscle I have aches."

"Well then, a stiff drink should sort you right out," Karen replied. "Miranda?"

"Yes, please," Miranda stared out the window. "I can't quite believe we're here. This is like some kind of fairy tale."

Karen nodded. "Sometimes I still can't believe it, either."

"More importantly, dreamers, what's for dinner?" Jodi bumped Karen's hip. "What gourmet feast have you prepared for us, oh food goddess?"

Karen bumped her back, her soft, round figure a charming contrast to Jodi's lithe, athletic build.

"Always thinking about food, aren't you? Mark thought we should fire up the barbecue tonight and have a big vegetarian smorgasbord out on the deck. James and Carly from down the street are coming—they're very interested in tennis and apparently have a thousand questions for you. I think James fancies himself as pro material, actually. And Cheryl Miller is coming too. You remember her from last time you were here?"

Jodi frowned and shook her head.

"She owns the café in town, you remember her—big red hair and quite loud? She was very impressed with you."

"Oh, yes," Jodi said dryly, recalling the large, enthusiastic woman with the shock of red hair. "She seemed to think my knee had been designated as a resting place for her hand."

Karen chuckled. "Well, I thought if we didn't invite her tonight and she found out you'd been here she might never serve me in the café again. We'll just have to seat you opposite her this time."

"Anything to keep the locals happy," Jodi said with a sweet smile. "Now, I could definitely use that drink."

The evening was perfect. The black sky mingled with the ocean and provided the perfect accompaniment to their simple meal and friendly conversation. The only way to tell where the ocean ended and the sky began was by the wash of bright stars.

Miranda fit into the group well and laughter flowed as abundantly as the wine.

Cheryl, from a safe distance across the table, amused the group with bawdy jokes and a quick sense of humor. By the time they had all scraped the last morsels of Karen's magnificent peach pie from their bowls, Jodi realized she was quite ready for bed. The strain on her body from the previous week, along with a little wine and a fun evening, had left her happily tired, and she was quite pleased when the guests began to take their leave. Jodi shook hands warmly all round, appreciative of the well wishes for her upcoming tournaments.

As the door finally closed behind Cheryl—who had insisted on hugging Jodi just a little too tightly, for just a little too long—Jodi yawned and leaned against the dark wooden door.

"I'm beat, you guys. Can we leave the dishes for morning?"

"What dishes?" Karen slipped an arm around Jodi's waist. "We had a barbecue. The only things to wash are the plates and they're in the dishwasher already!"

Jodi sighed. "Oh that's wonderful," she said. "We should eat more barbecues. So, does anyone mind if I go to bed?"

"Not at all," Karen gave her a squeeze. "We're quite okay here with Miranda, aren't we Mark? We have a lot of questions for her, actually."

"Hey, no fair," Jodi appealed, suddenly nervous about what they might drag out of Miranda if she went to bed. "Miranda, don't let them talk your ear off, okay?"

"I think I can manage," Miranda said with a grin. "You go.

I'm not quite ready for sleep. I want to look at these stars for a bit longer."

Jodi kissed Karen and Mark goodnight and nodded to Miranda as she made her way from the room. The realization that she and Miranda would share a bedroom that night set her belly aflutter.

"It's not like we're sharing a bed," Jodi muttered to herself. As she brushed her teeth, she noted the tired lines around her eyes and the slight pink in her cheeks from the sun. *I will not lose my head*, she thought. *We're sleeping in the same room for one night. Tomorrow we'll catch the plane home and life resumes. This is just a bit out of the ordinary. But I am excited to be sleeping in the same room as her.* She rubbed her face roughly with a towel. *Stop it.* She would think of the wildcard and go to bed.

Jodi lay on the firm little fold-out bed under a light summer sheet, comforted by the murmur of conversation from the other room as she stared out at the stars. She focused on her breathing as she'd been taught to do on the court, and tried to center herself; she needed to let go of the thoughts and feelings that clamored for her attention. Elated over her win, confused by the emotions stirred up by seeing her dad, and exhausted from the physical exertion of the tournament, Jodi drifted off to sleep. Sometime later, she awoke to the sounds of shuffling and Miranda quietly swearing.

Dazed, Jodi sat up.

"Shit," she heard a whisper in the darkness. Bright starlight outlined Miranda's figure.

"Are you okay?" Jodi mumbled, pushing herself up on her arm.

"Sorry, Jodi," Miranda whispered, "I'm so sorry to wake you. Go back to sleep, okay?"

"Okay." Jodi laid back down on her pillow and closed her eyes, dimly aware of Miranda's movements. "Wait, what's wrong?"

"I'm trying to sort out my bed."

"What's the matter with it?"

"It's deflated and I can't figure out how to blow it back up."

Jodi fumbled with the bedside lamp. She winced and shut her eyes tightly as bright light flared through the room. When she cracked open an eye she saw Miranda, dressed in a pair of short, boyish pajamas, crouched at the end of the sadly deflated blow-up bed.

"Sorry," Miranda apologized. "I woke up and the bed had gone so flat it was sucking me in to it. I think there's a valve or something here." She pulled at a tube sticking out from the bed. "I think I can blow it back up again."

Jodi watched Miranda put her lips to the valve and blow into it repeatedly. It was a losing proposition. The harder Miranda blew, the flatter the bed became.

"Shit," Miranda swore quietly again, only this time with more urgency.

"I think you need a pump or something for beds like that," Jodi said groggily.

"Yeah, I guess." Miranda stood up, hands on her hips as she stared at the bed. Resignedly, she dragged the sheet onto the floor and pushed the bed into the corner of the room.

"What are you doing?" Jodi yawned.

"I'm going to sleep on the floor."

Jodi eyed the thin sheet and the hard wooden floor. "You can't do that." She grabbed her pillow and wriggled as far over to one side of the small couch bed as she could. "Here, you can share with me."

"Oh, I couldn't! Don't worry, I'll be fine," Miranda protested. "Maybe there's a spare blanket or something in one of these cupboards." But when she pulled them open, they were empty.

"Miranda, don't be ridiculous. It's fine. Just come up here. It's the middle of the night and we can't fix this now, so let's just get some sleep."

"Are you sure?" Miranda's voice was uncertain.

"Yes, I'm sure. I don't snore and I don't even hog the bed, so let's just get some sleep now okay?"

"Okay."

Miranda paused and then slid quickly into the bed.

"Thanks, Jodi," she said quietly.

When Jodi flicked off the light, the room was once again bathed in starlight.

"It's no problem." Jodi closed her eyes but awareness of Miranda next to her made sleep difficult. Miranda shifted slightly and Jodi tried not to imagine how close they were in this little bed, with only a light sheet between them. She turned onto her back abruptly, and then turned again, trying to shake off the thoughts and find a comfortable position.

"Are you okay?" Miranda asked quietly.

Jodi turned to face Miranda. As her eyes adjusted to the dark she could see Miranda turned towards her, shadows from the night outside playing across her face.

"I guess," Jodi replied. Her heart beat loudly in her ears.

"You just 'guess'?" Miranda smoothed a wayward strand of Jodi's hair. "What's wrong?"

Jodi intertwined Miranda's fingers with her own and kissed them softly.

"It's hard to sleep with you this close," Jodi said in a thick voice.

"I think I know what you mean." Miranda leaned forward and kissed Jodi.

As their lips met Jodi felt alive, her mouth opening to deepen the kiss. She circled Miranda's palm with her thumb as their tongues slid against each other. Fragrant night air stole in through the open window. Miranda trailed her fingers down Jodi's back, setting off shivers across Jodi's skin. She could feel the delicious curves of Miranda's body under her light nightshirt as their bodies brushed against each other and the last traces of sleep left her. *So this is it*, she thought reverently. *This is what she feels like*. Jodi let go of Miranda's hand to pull her in closer, hooking her thumb under the waistband of Miranda's shorts.

"I want you," Jodi murmured, breaking the kiss for a moment to stare into Miranda's eyes.

Waves crashed against the dark cliffs outside their window as they gazed at each other, their room strangely lit up in the darkness by moon and starlight.

"You've got me."

Miranda suddenly captured Jodi's mouth, kissing her deeply. Her hand skimmed lightly over Jodi's ribs, pushing aside her shirt to brush fingertips lightly against the sensitive skin under Jodi's shirt. Jodi impatiently tugged her shirt off and reached for Miranda's.

"Take yours off too," she whispered urgently. "I want to feel you against me."

They lay facing each other in the soft shadows, Jodi breathless at the sight of Miranda's creamy skin, the perfect curve of her breast, the dip of her abdomen running under her shorts. She lowered her head to Miranda's breast, using her tongue to ignite spot fires of craving.

A loan gull called out from the cliffs below.

Jodi closed her eyes as Miranda impatiently reclaimed her mouth, slipping Jodi's shorts down as their bodies entwined under the soft summer sheet. A tiny voice in the back of her mind tried to remind Jodi that she had told herself she wouldn't do this. *As if I could stop it now.* Miranda's caresses drifted lower, sliding over Jodi's taught belly, into the warmth below, and all rationale disappeared. Her only thought was to have more, more of Miranda.

"Touch me now," Jodi said. "I need you to touch me."

She held Miranda tightly, hands skating over bare skin as they found each other in the semi-darkness. Miranda arched her back, pressing deeply against Jodi as a bead of sweat ran down between her breasts. Warm night air filled the room as they moved together, matching each other's rhythm, pulses quickening unbearably as they touched each other.

"Oh, god," Miranda whispered, her voice tight, "I'm going to—"

"Same," Jodi cried, feeling the world tilt slightly as she held on tightly to Miranda, cascading over the edge into orgasm.

And as the moon finally passed out of sight of their window they eventually slept, tangled in each other's arms.

CHAPTER FIFTEEN

Jodi awoke to the sound of voices in the hallway, the unfamiliar weight of Miranda's arm across her chest causing her a momentary sense of confusion. She shifted slightly, her sensitive bare skin singing with arousal as she felt Miranda's naked body pressed into her back.

Oh my God. Memory of the night they had just shared flooded in, causing her to throb. Jodi's eyes flew open and she winced at the bright sunshine streaming into the room. What had she done? Easing herself gingerly out of Miranda's arms, she slid gently out of the bed, holding her breath. She prayed Miranda wouldn't wake up. Grabbing her towel and some clothes from her bag she let herself quietly from the room and slipped across the narrow hallway to the bathroom.

Oh. My. God. Jodi sat on the edge of the deep, claw-foot bath, taking shaky breaths. That had not been meant to happen. What the hell am I going to do now? Her eyes flicked around the quaint little bathroom as if searching for answers in amongst the shelf of towel sets and lotions. She certainly couldn't just pretend it hadn't happened this time. It had been hard enough the last few weeks to ignore the kiss they had shared in Miranda's kitchen. But this—this was huge. Jodi sighed, leaning into the bath to turn on the shower taps. How had she let this happen? She'd promised herself she would focus on her tennis and not get caught up in any distractions.

She shivered as she waited for the water to run warm. Last night certainly had the power to become an enormous distraction, she decided, shedding her towel and climbing over the side of the bath to stand under the deluge. The showerhead was wide and the jet of water was strong. *Oh why did I do that?* Jodi soaped herself with a thick bar of soap that smelled faintly of vanilla, feeling suddenly weak as she remembered Miranda's hands on her. Miranda stroking her, Miranda kissing her, Miranda touching her until she was lost to herself. A sharp spasm of desire tugged at her and she groaned quietly, turning her face into the water. She briefly considered getting out of the shower and slipping back into the bed with Miranda. *But that would just make things even more complicated*, she thought. She turned off the hot tap, gasping as the shock of cold water hit her warm skin. Take a cold shower they say, she told herself grimly, quickly rinsing the soap from her body. She stood under the freezing water for as long as she could bear and then shut it off, rubbing herself briskly with the thick, scratchy towel.

I will have to talk to her. She sighed again as she looked at herself in the mirror for a moment, the dark lines under her eyes the only giveaway of a night spent barely sleeping. Perhaps her lips were a little redder, a little fuller, she thought, studying them as she leaned in closer. The crashing memory of her mouth, hot against Miranda's taut skin caused her to reel and she gripped the little white basin under the mirror. Clearly a cold shower was not going to cut it. Steeling herself, she got dressed quickly and headed back across the hallway. This was not going to be easy.

Miranda was standing by the window, already dressed in shorts and a soft, dark singlet, her back to the door.

"Miranda," Jodi said hesitantly.

Miranda turned slowly away from the view. Her hooded eyes seemed abnormally pale against the glittering blue of the sky and sea behind her.

"Miranda, we have to talk."

Miranda inclined her head, as if waiting to hear more. Neither of them moved towards the other across the room.

Jodi cleared her throat, nervously. "About last night." She waited for Miranda to speak, biting her lip anxiously. "I think it's best if we can just put it behind us," Jodi said quickly in the face of Miranda's continuing silence. Miranda's face was disconcertingly unreadable.

When she finally spoke, Miranda's tone was cool. "I thought you might say that."

"I really need to focus on my tennis," Jodi explained gently, feeling out of her depth. She had always avoided the difficult conversations in relationships, preferring to gloss over the top of things for the sake of peace. She took a deep breath and went on. "I can't afford any distractions right now, and stuff like this," Jodi looked around the room awkwardly, "well stuff like this just makes it impossible for me to concentrate. I'm sorry. I can't do this. I'm right on the verge of winning the wild card and I just have to focus on that."

Miranda's tight smile didn't reach her eyes. "It's okay Jodi, I understand how you feel. It was my mistake, not to mention completely unprofessional of me."

Jodi felt the gulf between them widen and wished she could shore it up, feeling helpless as Miranda turned back to stare out of the window.

"It was both of us, really," Jodi paused, realizing she sounded embarrassingly trite as the words came out of her mouth: "Can we be friends?"

Miranda gave a little laugh. "I wouldn't say friends exactly. But I'd like to stay on as your coach for now, if you're okay with that?"

"Yes, of course," Jodi rushed. "Of course I want you to stay on. Things are starting to really come together."

"That they are," Miranda replied wryly, stepping away from the window. Jodi stood in the doorway as Miranda moved purposely across the room to her bag. She rummaged through it. Jodi wasn't sure what to do with herself. She wanted to go to Miranda and hold her, to look into Miranda's eyes and find the connection she had just broken and patch it back up, but she didn't move. She couldn't. She swallowed painfully, her throat constricted.

Miranda pulled out her cell phone, not meeting Jodi's eyes. "I'm just going to pop out and make a phone call. I'm ready to go when you are. Just give me a shout when you're set."

Jodi stepped out of the doorway to let Miranda past, hugging her arms around herself to keep from reaching out. This is for the best, Jodi told herself, quelling the flood of protest inside her as she busied herself in the room. She repacked her bag and straightened the bed, knowing Karen and Mark would probably just strip it anyway, but she wanted to do something. She forced herself not to think about last night as she pulled the sheet up and fixed the pillows, faltering for a moment when she caught the subtle scent of Miranda's perfume. Jodi sat on the side of the bed, feeling the springs shift beneath her weight as she stared unseeingly before her. I'm doing the right thing here, she told herself, trying to ignore the heavy feeling in heart.

Miranda stepped quickly out of the house, pressing the phone hard against her ear. She smiled brightly at Mark who was bringing some bags in from the car. Her heart skipped painfully as she mouthed "phone call" to him, and slipped past him to head down the drive.

The quiet purr of her own home phone ringing accompanied her as she walked quickly, gravel crunching beneath her feet. She imagined the sound of the ring in her empty house, Eddie curled up on the couch turning an ear lazily towards the bell. When she felt she was safely out of sight of the house she hung up and stopped walking, dropping the phone into her pocket.

She took a deep breath, filling her nostrils with the scent of the morning. Sun-kissed wildflowers tangled by the side of the road, their flashes of white and orange startling against the long green grass. The blue of the sky was so perfect, the day so sweet, she almost couldn't bear it. She came across a low, dilapidated wooden bench, which she decided must have once been a bus stop; she stopped and sat, and put her head in her hands as the tears she had been holding back finally spilt over.

What a fool I am, she thought, scuffing her foot against the grass. Memories of the previous night crowded her mind; desire and embarrassment fought each other for first place. Jodi had crooked her finger and she, Miranda, had come running, only to be sent packing at first light. She knew how Jodi felt about her tennis right now. She had known as she slid into the bed with her that Jodi had no room in her life for a girlfriend, no time for love. Jodi had made that absolutely clear after they had kissed in Miranda's kitchen.

Miranda had thought her feelings were under control. Some control, she thought bleakly, as she watched a trail of ants march over the grass. It's lonely, she realized, always being on the road, with no one to hold at night, no one to wake up with. At home with her garden and her cat and her best friend close by, Miranda hadn't noticed there was a gap in her life. She had had her fair share of dates and short relationships, but no one had really captured her attention, content as she was with the easy life she had built for herself. But since she had met Jodi, if she was honest with herself, her heart had been crying out for more.

She had opted out of the double dates Enid had tried to organize, protesting that she was too busy as she waved off Enid's insistence that she would end up an old maid. Well, I am too busy, she thought crossly, thinking of the hectic schedule they kept, racing to tournaments and practice sessions across the country. *But not too busy to make love with Jodi.*

Wearily, she stood up. She knew she needed to get back so that they could make their flight. She was thankful to be returning home today, glad to know she could retreat to her own space where Jodi couldn't reach her, where she could fall apart and put herself back together in privacy. Maybe we're both just lonely, she thought, as she made her way back down the road to the house. But she knew that was lying to herself. Miranda fought off the wave of shame that threatened to overcome her as she remembered waking up alone in the little pull-out bed, well aware that Jodi would regret their night together. She wished she didn't have to go back to the house this morning.

Rounding a corner, she stopped for a moment to take in the magnificent view of fresh morning ocean spray, jetting up against the granite cliffs. Her heart twisted painfully as she remembered catching the sound of the ocean the night before, in amongst their muted cries as they had held each other breathtakingly close. *But she doesn't want me like that. She wants me to be her coach—at least until Jase is back on board.* Well, she vowed, I will be the most professional coach on the circuit from now on. Her resolve was fierce. It doesn't matter what it is—loneliness, lust— Miranda shook off the thought before it could go any further. It didn't matter. She started again back towards the house. As soon as Jase can take over I'll go back to the Juniors. I can't stay on with Jodi.

"Right. Are we ready?" Jason slid his laptop onto the table and flipped open the lid.

"No. But let's find out anyway." Jodi stretched forward in her seat, leaning her elbows on the table.

After all they'd been through together, Miranda was surprised she didn't feel more nervous, as they sat together around the plastic table in the clubhouse, waiting for the laptop to fire up. The final rankings were due to be released at ten. If Jodi was at the top, the wildcard would be hers. Miranda glanced at the clubhouse clock; its large green display showed five minutes to ten. She waited to feel something, anything at all—a small flip of her stomach, a quickening of her heartbeat— but she felt nothing. She had been feeling oddly numb for the last few weeks.

Miranda had cried upon her return from Vancouver, burying her head in Eddie's soft fur as she tried to let go of the hurt. She had sobbed herself to sleep, holding on to Eddie like a lifeline. In the morning, Eddie had disentangled himself and walked away, giving her a reproachful look as he settled himself at a respectful distance, licking himself purposefully. The morning sun was hard on her raw eyes as she propped herself up on an elbow and looked at her cat.

"You're right Eddie," she said to him. "I need to pull myself together." And so she had gotten up, washed her face and busied herself around the house. *What will be, will be*, she told herself through gritted teeth as she pushed the vacuum cleaner determinedly across the kitchen floor. There was no possibility of anything further between her and Jodi—Jodi had made that crystal clear and Miranda was not willing to risk making a further fool of herself by trying to pursue it.

Her arm ached as she scrubbed her kitchen sink mercilessly, bringing out its metallic shine. She tried to imagine what she would have done in Jodi's position. Would she have been so one track, so intensely focused on her career if she had had the chances Jodi had? Or would she have been able to be more balanced, and let's face it, she thought to herself ruefully, *more human*. It was hard for her to put herself in Jodi's position. Sweeping a cloth over the glass on the oven door she stood back to admire her handy work. The kitchen gleamed back at her, but she didn't feel satisfied. An emptiness gnawed at her stomach, and she briefly considered stopping for a snack, but decided to move on. She didn't feel like eating. She felt like cleaning.

Hours later she stood in the bath, the shower beating down on her as she scrubbed the tiles clean. *Would I have been different?* The question was plaguing her. She knew it was impossible to pull it all apart– to understand Jodi in terms of what her own decisions might have been was useless, really, and her mind ached from trying. Suddenly feeling weak, she sat down on the floor of the bath, gulping down sobs as the water ran down her face. *What a fool I've been*. If Jodi loved her, nothing else would have mattered. She was using her tennis career as an excuse to avoid any real connection with Miranda and Miranda felt stupid for having only just realized. *And I've gone and fallen in love with her*. Well, she thought, standing up wearily and shutting off the shower, I will just have to *unfall* in love with her.

So she had swallowed it down, like the painfully large pill that it was, and forced herself to try to move on. But the quiet coldness that settled around her heart felt unfamiliar and strange.

Miranda had gone through the motions with Jodi over the last few weeks, helping her train for the final tournament, cheering from the stands as Jodi had accepted the winner's trophy, smiling and shaking hands incessantly at the parties that followed, and slipping out at the first opportunity to escape to the sanctuary of her home. She had felt like she was seeing it all through someone else's eyes, watching herself do and say all the right things, knowing she wasn't quite there. Thankfully Sal's pregnancy complications had finally cleared up and Jase was back in full swing. She would speak to him this week about leaving the team.

Jodi shifted again in the seat next to her, clearly anxious as they waited for the website to load.

"Will there be an official letter or something? If Jodi gets the wildcard?" Miranda asked, bringing her attention back to the table.

"Yeah," Jason tapped in his login details and password, connecting them to the official site. "But we'll be able to tell anyway from today's rankings. Okay, the file's up."

Jason clicked on a link and the file loaded up, filling the browser. They followed together as Jason scrolled down past the men's rankings to the women's list. He gave a loud whoop as they saw Jodi's name, clearly printed in neat, black type at the top of the official list.

"Oh my God, Jodi! You did it!" Jason jumped up from the table, throwing his hands into his hair. He leaned back, crowing with excitement. "Top of the list!" he shouted.

Jodi let out a shaky breath, her face breaking into a grin.

"I did it," she said quietly.

"Congratulations, Jodi," Miranda smiled warmly at her. "You've definitely earned it."

"I can't believe it," Jodi repeated, clearly in shock.

"You better believe it," Jason whooped again. "You got the card, Jodes. US Open, here we come!"

"I honestly just can't believe it," Jodi said again, shaking her head as she stared at the computer. Miranda watched as a mixture of relief and disbelief fought for first place on Jodi's face, catching the shine of what she thought might even have been tears in her eyes.

"Thank you both so much. I couldn't have done it without you." Jodi looked from Jason to Miranda. "You've both been amazing." Her gaze rested on Miranda, an unreadable expression in her eyes. Miranda felt her breath catch, wondering what she was going to say.

"We're a good team," Jason broke in, thumping the table with excitement. "It's onwards and upwards from here, Jodi. Now, we've got to get planning. We've only got three weeks."

Jodi laughed, breaking eye contact with Miranda. "No rest for the wicked."

CHAPTER SIXTEEN

Jason looked helplessly at Miranda from across his desk.

"I can't say I understand your decision." His brow wrinkled, announcing his confusion. "You're sure this is what you want?"

"Yes."

"Explain it to me one more time?"

Miranda sighed. "I want to go back to the Juniors. Now that you're back on board with Jodi you can see her through the US Open. You guys don't need me, and I'd really like to get back involved with the Juniors."

"You're right Miranda. We don't *need* you. But I thought we were working so well as a team. I'd really like you to stay on board, and I know Jodi would. You're invaluable as a hitting partner and you've really shown your skills these last few weeks, covering for me. I don't understand this."

Miranda bit her lip, unsure how to go on. She didn't want to say the wrong thing and expose herself or Jodi to any further awkwardness, but she knew she had to pull herself from the team. She hadn't been feeling right in her own skin and she knew needed to get away from Jodi to sort herself out. She needed some space to clear her head and calm her heart.

"I'm sorry Jase, I don't mean to let you down. I just think it's better for me right now to be in a less pressured environment. I know I can do well with the Juniors, I've proved that, and I'd like to be in a position where I can perform at my best."

"Don't you want to advance your career?"

Miranda shrugged. Yes, she thought, fussing with a paperclip on the desk in front of her. *Yes, I really do.* "I guess it's just not as important to me as I'd thought."

"And there's nothing else wrong? You can talk to me, you know?" Concern laced his voice.

"I know, Jase. Thank you, but really, there's nothing else. I just feel like I'm better suited to the Juniors. I only just pulled it over the line for Jodi in Vancouver and I totally dropped the ball in Austin. I'd hate to muck anything up for her now that the stakes are so high, so it's really better for everyone if I can just go back to the Juniors." She could hear the note of pleading in her voice.

Jason blew out a tight sigh. "You didn't muck anything up Miranda. How many times do I have to tell you? You really do win some and lose some."

"I know, I know" she reassured him. "Please Jase?"

He gathered together some paperwork on his desk, clearly not happy with her request. "I'll have to shuffle some things around."

"I'd really appreciate that."

"If you're absolutely sure."

"I am," Miranda nodded emphatically.

"Okay then."

The afternoon's heat was the kind that cracked sidewalks and melted roads. An impossibly blue sky gave little sign of the weather bureau's predicted thunderstorm. Miranda walked around the court, scooping up balls with her racket, flicking them expertly into the trolley. With the last ball secured away, she stood for a moment, adjusting her cap against the glare of the relentless sun as she gazed at the clubhouse. She had had a good solid session with the Juniors today and then sent them off to the pool for a couple of hours of well-deserved fun. Some of them were already proving themselves to be winners, taking the matches in the first rounds of their tournaments with ease. She was proud of their eager faces and desire for excellence.

Miranda pushed the ball trolley in front of her with her racket, knowing the metal would be too hot to touch by now, having been out in the sun for the last few hours. She wondered how Jodi and Jason were doing. The first rounds of the US Open were due to start next week and she knew they would be training hard and strategizing feverishly. At first, Miranda had been anxious that she might bump in to Jodi at the clubhouse, but with the Juniors mostly training in the afternoons, she had managed to avoid that embarrassment for the last two weeks. Knowing Jodi liked to train first thing in the morning, Miranda had stayed away from the clubhouse until later in the day, doing paperwork from home in the mornings and then working with Junior groups from lunchtime into the late summer evenings.

Miranda opened the equipment shed, and nudged the trolley in front of her into its oven- like heat. The room felt like a sauna; the corrugated iron had absorbed and trapped the unbearable warmth and she felt sweat immediately begin to coat her skin. She quickly maneuvered the ball trolley into the corner and grabbed a bundle of rackets from the repairs shelf to be restrung.

"Miranda!" The voice made her jump as she turned to leave the shed. She spilled the rackets to the floor with a clatter. A silhouette blocked the doorway. The brilliant sunshine behind made it difficult to see the face, but the voice was unmistakably Jodi's.

Miranda bent down to gather up the rackets, "Phew! Hey, you gave me a fright."

"Sorry," Jodi replied softly. "You need a hand?"

Miranda straightened up, hugging the rackets close to her chest. "I'm all right, thanks."

"I didn't mean to scare you. I was just coming in to grab some balls—I'm going to hit some serves."

"But it's the afternoon. You're not supposed…" Miranda faltered. "I mean, you don't usually train here in the afternoons." She cringed inwardly. Nice one, Miranda, she thought. This heat is addling my brain.

Jodi raised an eyebrow. "I felt like working on some serves…. if that's okay with you?"

"Of course," Miranda stammered. "Sorry. Here, let me get out of your way."

Miranda stepped out of the shed, glad to be out of the broiling hot box. She knew her face would be flushed, red and sweaty, her pale hair pasted against her neck. Of all the times to bump into Jodi. Naturally, the heat didn't seem to be affecting Jodi. She was gorgeous as usual. Her clear, tanned skin looked cool in the sweltering day. Her hair was pulled back from her face, exposing the graceful sweep of her long neck and toned shoulders. Miranda closed her eyes for a second, overcome by the memory of her own hands on those shoulders, her lips on that delicious, soft skin.

"Miranda? Are you okay?" Jodi's voice was low with concern and Miranda's eyes flew open.

"I'm fine. It was just so hot in there."

"Are you sure?" Jodi took a step closer and Miranda felt her heart jump.

"Really, I'm fine." Miranda edged back, widening the distance between them.

"So, how's it all going with the Juniors?" Jodi asked carefully.

"Oh, it's really great. They're really coming into themselves," Miranda said and smiled in spite of herself. "They challenge me, but I like their fresh ideas and passion."

Jodi nodded, smiling as well. "I remember being a Junior. The world feels amazing when you're at that age. Full of promise and so…" She seemed to search for a word: "Conquerable."

Miranda grinned. "I felt that way, too. Maybe that's why I can relate to them so well."

"You played Junior tournaments? Jase mentioned you had been in the Juniors but I didn't know you'd actually qualified for tournaments. No wonder you're such a good player."

"Yeah," Miranda looked away, her gaze travelling to the courts.

"What happened?"

Miranda felt her eyes cloud over. "I got sick."

"I'm sorry, I didn't know," Jodi said quietly, concern written on her face.

"It's okay." Miranda shrugged. "It was a while ago now. I'm more than over it."

"What happened? Do you mind me asking?"

"When I was seventeen," Miranda paused, bringing her gaze back to Jodi's face, "I got cancer. I had to stop playing for a few years. By the time I could return to the court my fitness had gone, my edge was lost and it was too late for me." She smiled ruefully. "I drifted around for a few years and finally found my way back to tennis through coaching."

"Wow." Jodi paused, as if to take it all in. "That must have been hard."

"It was. But I love tennis, and I'm glad with all that I am to be back here. And I don't want to do anything to jeopardize that," Miranda said, surprising herself with a small flare of anger. Jodi hadn't been the only one with interests to protect. She herself had risked her position at the club with hardly a thought.

"I understand."

Miranda caught the undertone of meaning in Jodi's voice.

"I'm sure you do. Well, I'd better get these rackets off to be re-strung."

"Would you like to hit some balls with me before you go?"

"Oh, I…" Miranda trailed off, looking at her watch, "I really can't. I've got to get these in before five o'clock or they won't be ready for tomorrow's session."

"Of course," Jodi smiled—Miranda thought—a little wistfully.

"I could do it another time, if you need a hitting partner, that is. You've got Steven now though, right?" Miranda's attempt to sound casual came out awkwardly, even to her own ears. She had struggled with the decision to call Jodi and personally let her know she wasn't going to continue on the team, but in the end she had taken the cowardly way out, deciding that Jason had employed her so she only really needed to tell Jason. She had convinced herself that it was the best decision, but now, standing before Jodi, she regretted it. She should have called Jodi and told her personally. Well, it's too late to say something now, Miranda thought.

"Yeah, Steven is great. It's all good, I just thought if you were free now we could have a hit, but you're busy, so don't worry." Jodi took a step forward, her dark eyes serious. "Miranda, about Vancouver, I'm sorry, I-"

"Please don't." Miranda cut in, her heart lurching. The last thing she needed right now was another explanation from Jodi about why she didn't want to be with her. "Please, let's just put it behind us. We've both agreed it was a mistake and I think we've said all we need to say on that." She took a step backwards, shifting the weight of the rackets in her arms.

Jodi studied her face for a moment, her voice quiet as she simply said, "Okay."

Miranda paused, feeling uncertain. She wanted to say more but felt unsure of what to say. Surely Jodi could understand? It was simply too painful to go back over it all again.

"I'd better let you go," Jodi said, nodding towards the bundle of rackets. "See you around, Miranda."

"I… good luck for next week." Clutching the rackets, Miranda backed away and turned in the direction of the repair shop. Don't look back, she counseled herself. Just keep walking.

Jodi watched Miranda leave. Her heart constricted painfully at the sight of the straight line of Miranda's back, the swing of her blonde hair turned golden under the sun. Two weeks apart had left an ache of longing that had turned into a roar the moment she had seen Miranda head into the equipment shed. Jodi wasn't supposed to have been there this afternoon. She had come on a whim, telling herself she needed to do some more work on her serve, ignoring the little voice inside her that protested, insisting she had already trained hard enough in the morning.

Grabbing the ball trolley, Jodi wheeled it out of the shed into the afternoon sun. She couldn't deny that she missed

Miranda. Was that what she had been going to tell her? The words had begun to tumble out of her, almost of her own accord. She wondered where she might have ended up if Miranda had not cut her off. She missed working with Miranda. She missed Miranda's words of encouragement, her well-timed pieces of advice, and even her little dances of glee when she managed to return one of Jodi's particularly difficult shots. Jodi found she kept looking for Miranda across the court when she was training, but the serious face of Steven, her new assistant coach, was a stark reminder of Miranda's absence. Jodi wanted to talk with her after training, to grab a water and head to the shower blocks, to chat and laugh easily about everything and nothing. She missed Miranda's face first thing in the morning, coffee in hand, waiting by the courts for their first training session. She missed their shared lunches and "dinners of war," the nickname they had given their evening strategy sessions.

Jason's news had felt like a slap, but she had accepted it with a shrug. Jodi knew he had wanted to ask more but thankfully he hadn't and she hadn't offered up anything further. What more could she say? Jodi had basically made it impossible for Miranda to stay, and whilst she was hurt by the news, she couldn't say she was surprised. Jodi found herself training harder than she ever had before. She threw herself physically and mentally into the game, leaving no room for anything but tennis. And yet still, as she would crawl exhausted into bed at the end of the day, a picture of Miranda's bright, smiling face would flash behind her tired eyes. And as she drifted off to sleep, her pillow would be wet with tears.

Jodi was frustrated with herself. Where's my self-control, she thought as she set herself up to serve on the court. Thumping a ball across the net she tried to calm her mind, but she couldn't shake the vision of Miranda standing before her, all rosy cheeked and desirable.

She hadn't known Miranda had been sick. *Whack.* She sent another ball flying across the court, pushing herself harder than ever. Why hadn't she known that? They had known each other for almost two months now; they had traveled together across the country, and spent more time together than Jodi had spent with anyone since she had broken up with Tara. I didn't even spend this much time with Tara in the last few years, she acknowledged ruefully. *You didn't know because you didn't ask.* Jodi smashed a ball wildly out of the court, cursing as she lined up again. *You're too focused on yourself.* She gritted her teeth, trying to ignore the voice inside her. The words were only punishing because they were true.

Well, it's too late now she thought, crossing to the other side of the court with the ball trolley. When she hadn't heard a word from Miranda for over a week, she had started to feel uneasy. She hadn't expected Miranda to leave the team. She had known it might be awkward between them as they tried to move on from Vancouver, but she had thought they could get past it. But now, obviously, their professional relationship was done, and so was their fragile, yet budding friendship. *Some friendship.* I didn't even know anything about her. Slamming a ball ferociously into the net, Jodi cried out in frustration as a pinch of pain ran up her side. Dejectedly, she dropped her racket, knowing that to go on would be pushing things too far. She sat for a moment on the bluestone wall at the edge of the court, and let her head fall into her hands. What had she been going to say to Miranda, she wondered. She didn't even know. She just knew she missed her.

Jodi rubbed her eyes tiredly. She had won the wildcard. The official letter had come in the mail, and she had stuck it on the fridge in her hotel room with a quick thrill of pride. She had won. And yet the dull ache she constantly felt inside her told her she had also lost, utterly and completely.

CHAPTER SEVENTEEN

"Enid, you have to come to this party with me, I cannot go alone," Miranda begged, desperately hoping Enid would take pity on her.

"But what about Abby? We were supposed to go out tonight." Enid didn't sound convinced.

"Bring her too, I don't care. We'll go all together. I just can't face this night on my own."

"Miranda," Enid sighed impatiently on the phone. "What's the problem? It's a party at your own clubhouse, for Pete's sake. You'll know everyone there."

"It's a party for Jodi."

"And?"

"And I need back-up. Everyone will be there to celebrate her getting the wildcard and they'll start asking me why I'm not on the team anymore and I can't bear it."

"So you think having Abby and I there to hold your hand will make it better?"

"Exactly."

"It won't, Miranda. They'll ask you anyway, and if they don't ask you tonight, they'll ask you the next time they see you. You just need to stay calm and tell them it's because you're in love with Jodi."

"Enid!" Miranda spluttered indignantly. "I am *not* in love with Jodi." She hadn't been able to bring herself to bare her broken heart to Enid. Enid was so happy with Abby, in the honeymoon flush of their new relationship, that Miranda hadn't felt like bringing down the mood. "Anyway," she continued stoically, "I'm over all that and you know it."

"Okay, okay, sorry! Just tell them what you told Jason," continued Enid. "The pressure was too much for you, tell them you missed your Juniors. Two seconds later, it'll be old news."

"So you won't come?"

"It's not that I *won't* come, I just don't think it will make things better for you. It will look weird if you turn up to Jodi's party with a couple of strangers."

"But you're not strangers—she knows you."

"Yes, but it's not like we're all great friends from way back. Go to the party, Miranda. Stay for an hour or so and sneak out. No one will notice," Enid advised.

"So you're abandoning me."

Enid chuckled. "I'm not abandoning you. I'm helping you to grow up."

"Well, if this is growing up, it's stupid."

"Yes, well, growing up is definitely stupid. Now ring me afterwards and come and find us. We're going to that new bar on 57th."

Miranda checked herself in the mirror one more time, smoothed her hair into place and adjusted her shirt. After rejecting everything in her wardrobe at least twice, she had eventually settled on a pair of slim black pants and a sailor-striped shirt. She eyed herself critically for a moment, trying to imagine how others would see her. She knew she was pretty; she'd certainly had her fair share of offers in noisy bars and clubs, based on what could only be looks, but tonight she couldn't seem to see herself that way. In her reflection, she could only see herself in parts: large blue eyes, overly wide mouth, and slightly crooked nose. She felt like a puzzle she had forgotten how to put back together. She took a deep breath, trying to breathe some life into her aching heart. *Come on*, she willed herself, *get over this please.*

Her phone buzzed in her pocket, startling her out of her reverie. She glanced at the display. "Enid? Changed your mind?" Miranda asked hopefully.

"I don't think so. Are you there yet? Why are you answering your phone?"

"I haven't left yet."

"Miranda! You're supposed to be there. Get out of the bathroom and get into your car!"

"Wait! How did you—" Miranda laughed, suddenly not surprised that her best friend had known she would be in the bathroom panicking over what to wear.

"Because I just know. Now get going. You're going to be late."

"Okay, okay! I'm leaving now." Miranda rang off, shaking her head. "Off you go then," she muttered to herself as she opened the closet door. She chose a light jacket and slipped it over her shoulders. "You'll have a great time."

Wishing she believed it, she clattered down the stairs, calling goodbye to Eddie as she slammed the front door shut

The little clubhouse was packed to the rafters with well-wishers. Apparently every man and his dog had come to celebrate Jodi's wildcard win and wish her luck for the Open. Pushing open the doors to the club, Miranda swore silently, realizing it would have been absolutely fine for her to bring Enid and Abby. As it was, she barely recognized most of the crowd.

Miranda ducked under an enormous, slightly askew, *good luck* sign adorning the entrance and, spying a drinks table, made her way through the crowd to snag a glass of wine. She would need at least one of those to make it through the evening. Balloons and tinsel hung from the ceiling, and the annual Christmas party decorations brightened up the room.

"Miranda! Hi!" A group of her Juniors rushed towards her, their faces alight with excitement.

"Hi Jessie, Becca, Thomas. Hi Nathan. You made it, huh?"

"Oh my God, we wouldn't miss this for the world." Jessie beamed, her smile a match for those of her fellow players.

"I can't believe she's going to the US Open," Becca squeaked. "I'm so excited I could pop. It's my dream, you know," she sighed, her eyes far away. "One day I'm going to win the US Open."

"Same," Thomas added, his voice breaking lightly as he grinned, self-conscious of his uncontrollably teen-aged voice box.

"Me too, bro," Nathan joined in, high-fiving Thomas.

Miranda smiled indulgently. "Well if you're all going to win it, I hope you won't have to play each other. I won't know who to cheer for."

The youngsters looked at each other uncertainly for a moment. "We can all just win it in different years!" Jessie announced, inspiring a round of happy *yeahs* and fist bumps.

"I hope we get to meet her," Becca said. "Can you introduce us, Miranda?"

"Introduce you to whom?" The voice over Miranda's shoulder caused her heart to skip a beat. She whirled around and came face-to-face with Jodi, stunning in a rakish black cowboy shirt and her trademark black jeans. Her hair was out, softly framing her face, falling long and straight down her back, her dark eyes dancing with amusement.

"Jodi! Uh, we were just talking about you. Good timing."

"Oh my God! It's her!" Becca squealed, squeezing forward and elbowing Miranda out of the way. "Ms. Richards, I'm a huge fan."

Jodi laughed, and reached out a hand to steady Miranda, in danger of toppling over a potted plant as the Juniors crowded forward.

"Whoa, guys," Miranda cried, finding her feet with a grin at Jodi. "Let's all just take a step back. Now, Jodi, these are some of my Juniors: Becca, Jessie, Thomas and Nathan. Guys, this is Jodi."

"We're so please to meet you, Ms. Richards." Jodi shook hands with each of the eagerly waiting teenagers. "We're all big fans of yours and we just know you're going to win the Open."

"Wow! Thanks, guys. Call me Jodi, please." Jodi gave them a wide smile. "Actually, I'm probably one of the least likely players to win it this year! At this stage I'm hoping just to make it to Round Four, which as you know would be a pretty great start." The Juniors nodded at her seriously, pleased to be given an insight into her plans. "But what's great," Jodi went on, "is that now that I've made it in to the US Open I can start doing the other big grand slams and my ranking will stay high. And who knows," she looked around at their enthusiastic faces, "maybe one day I'll win it."

"Yeah, you will!" Nathan cried, his face full of enthusiasm.

"You'll have to watch out though, Jodi," Miranda added with mock seriousness, "these guys have all set their sights on winning the US Open trophy too, so you'll have to win it soon if you don't want one of my Juniors to beat you to the punch."

Jodi's eyes twinkled as she grinned at the group. "I can already tell I'm going to have some stiff competition here. I tell you what, how about I come by one afternoon and have a hit with you when I'm done with the Open?" She turned questioning eyes to Miranda. "If that's okay with your coach?"

"Of course it's okay with her, isn't it Miranda?" Jessie chimed in quickly, her face shining with excitement.

"Of course," Miranda nodded, pleased for her players to be receiving such attention. She knew this would make their night, and the promise of playing with a pro like Jodi would fuel their continuing fire for excellence. "That would be great, Jodi."

"Jodi, there you are!" The unmistakably silken tones of Lisa Sevonny's voice cut through their conversation as the ever-gorgeous publicist stepped up beside Jodi, wrapping an arm around her waist.

"Darling, you simply must come with me, I've got about a hundred people lined up waiting to wish you good luck."

Miranda thought she saw a flicker of irritation cross Jodi's face, but decided she had been wrong when Jodi politely acquiesced. Jodi said a graceful goodbye to the Juniors, who wished her luck and reminded her of her promise to come and train with them one day.

Miranda watched Jodi go, noting Lisa's proprietorial hand resting on her back and wondered if things had changed between them. It was obvious that Lisa wanted Jodi. Had Jodi finally succumbed to the charms of the seriously good-looking, if a little bitchy, publicist?

"Come with us, Miranda," Becca cried, grabbing her hand. "There's actually an ice sculpture at the back of the room and it pumps out lemonade. You've got to try it."

Miranda laughed and allowed herself to be towed across the room in the enthusiastic little group. At least now she had seen Jodi and it hadn't been too terrible. She could stay for another hour and then slip out unnoticed.

* * *

An hour later Miranda found herself being shouted at by a fellow coach who was attempting to converse with her against the competing noise of the crowd and the DJ, who had seemingly sprung from nowhere to blast them with party tunes. She had mostly lost track of their conversation but breaking away seemed a bit rude. Suddenly, the music stopped, catching her companion short as he continued to shout.

"Oh," he said, as a quick blush rose up his neck. "The music's stopped." They laughed awkwardly together.

Jason's voice boomed out through the loudspeakers commanding the attention of the room.

"Ladies and Gentlemen." Jason grinned at the crowd. "Thank you all for coming tonight to celebrate with us. Here at the Sacramento Tennis Club, we sure know how to support our own, and you guys are definitely showing that support tonight for our one and only US Open entrant, Ms. Jodi Richards."

At the mention of Jodi's name, the crowd erupted into wild cheers. Jason waited for the noise to die down before he continued. "Tonight we're not going to carry on with a bunch of speeches until you're all falling asleep in your drinks, so, without further ado, I'd like to hand the microphone over to the lady herself. Please welcome Ms. Jodi Richards."

In a hail of stomping and cheering, Jodi stepped up to the podium, looking as poised as ever. Quiet confidence seemed to radiate from her as she looked over the crowd. Her face suddenly broke into a wide smile. "Well, aren't you all a rowdy bunch!"

The crowd laughed and clapped, as some wolf-whistled and called out encouragements.

"But seriously," Jodi said, as she leaned closer to the microphone, "I want to thank you all for coming to tonight's celebration. But it's not just about tonight. I want to thank you all for coming out to the matches, day after day, and for sitting in the sun for hours on end to watch us smash a tiny ball across the court at each other. I don't know quite why we do what we do, but I know that I love it and I just want to keep on doing it."

The crowd roared with appreciation as Jodi surveyed the room. "Most of you know Jason Stovak, my esteemed and fabulous coach. I couldn't have done this without him. Jase has been on my team for the long haul, literally through thick and thin, and by thin, I mean the years when I wasn't even here." Jodi stopped to grin, acknowledging the laughter in the audience. "But I'm back now, and I'm doing my damnedest to stay back. I'd also like to thank Miranda Ciccone, who some of you know has been training hard with me for the last few months, and who is now leading the Juniors to certain victory on the courts this season."

Miranda clutched her wine glass firmly, smiling through the applause. She felt a rush of gratitude to have been mentioned.

"And finally I'd like to thank all of you here at the clubhouse. I wish you all could come with me to New York for the Open!"

The music cut back in as Jodi stepped off the podium, shaking hands left and right with her admirers. Miranda took a deep breath. She was relieved Jodi had made it sound like she hadn't just quit.

Unexpectedly, tears pricked her eyes, and she took a gulp of her wine; she decided that now would be a good time to slip out. She skirted around the back of the crowd and ducked out the side exit, nodding at the groups of party-goers who had spilled out of the clubhouse and onto the courts. A desolate sadness rose up inside her as she made her way to her car. She knew, with a certain finality, that it was all really over. She would not be going with Jodi to New York; she was no longer a part of the team. Like everyone else, Miranda would have to wait and watch from the sidelines to find out how things were going. She wouldn't be there to watch Jodi's face concentrating carefully on a game plan, or to share a tired smile in the backseat on the way home from a match. There would be no more early morning hotel breakfasts and late night pow wows before bed. She wouldn't know when Jodi was worried or frustrated, or feeling insecure. She had forfeited her right to know and now she had to get used to being just like everyone else.

At her car she patted her pockets, looking for her keys. With a sigh of frustration she remembered they were in the pocket of her jacket, which was hanging snuggly on the back of a chair in the clubhouse.

"Dammit!" Miranda moaned. Wearily, she trudged back across the courts to the party. The DJ was obviously taking her role seriously, she thought, as the thump of the bass line spread out into the night. Miranda let herself back in the side door and made a beeline for her jacket, relieved to see it hanging just where she'd left it. She snagged it, hooking it over her arm as she felt for the keys in the pocket.

"Going so soon?" Jodi's voice carried above the music. Miranda grinned sheepishly, startled to find Jodi standing in front of her.

"It's past my bedtime," she said, raising her voice as Lady Gaga blared from the speakers.

Jodi cocked an eyebrow. She leaned in closer to be heard above the music, saying "Is it now? I seem to remember you were the one who liked to stay up late to chat."

Miranda caught Jodi's gaze and held it, not sure if it was her heart or the music hammering in her chest. "I don't know what I like anymore," she heard herself say as Jodi leaned in closer to catch her words.

"Drink darling? I hate to interrupt your tete-a-tete, but I almost had to break an arm to get these." Lisa's high laugh tinkled uncomfortably between them as she handed a glass of champagne to Jodi. Jodi took it, as if on auto-pilot, tearing her eyes slowly away from Miranda. With a wrench in her gut, Miranda watched Lisa drape an arm around Jodi's shoulder, pulling her in close. She needed to get out of here. It was one thing to quit the team and suffer in silence, knowing she would never see Jodi again. It was quite another to have to watch Jodi parade around with her lover. Did she not think Miranda had any feelings at all?

"Have a great night guys," Miranda managed, her voice tight in her throat. "I'd better go. Best of luck Jodi." She turned and fled from the room.

Grateful for the fresh air and space, the music followed Miranda as she pushed open the door to the short veranda. Her head was spinning and she grabbed the railing for a moment to steady herself before jogging down the stairs.

How do I get myself into these things, she wondered, glancing up at the stars as she walked back to her car. *I just wanted to be a coach.* Her heart ached like a freshly skinned knee. *I shouldn't have come tonight. I don't want to see her with someone else. I don't want to see her at all.* Miranda fumbled with her keys through a sheen of tears, trying to open the car door.

"Miranda, wait!" Miranda turned to see Jodi running towards the car. Miranda shook her head, determined to avoid any further pain for the evening. "Please, just wait a minute." Jodi threw her arm in front of the car door, blocking Miranda's way. "Miranda, please," she repeated.

"What, why?" Miranda hugged her arms around herself as if she could somehow protect herself from what was to come. She took a step backward. "What more can there be?"

"I- I didn't want you to get the wrong idea," Jodi stammered.

"The wrong idea about what?"

"About Lisa. About me and Lisa. I don't know why she's been acting like she owns me all night, but we're not seeing each other."

Miranda shrugged helplessly, "Okay."

"Just okay?"

"Well, yeah." Miranda blew out a sigh and toyed with her keys. "I said okay. I don't know why you're telling me. It's not like it's any of my business."

Jodi took a step forward, closing the gap between them.

"Do you want it to be your business?"

"What the hell, Jodi?" Miranda exploded, making no attempt to disguise her anger. "Why do you need to make me say it? You've been perfectly clear about where you stand. So what is this now, some kind of game for you? What are you looking for? Advantage: Richards?" Miranda jutted out her chin in frustration. "Well, you got what you wanted, so maybe you can just back away from the car and let me get on with my life now, please."

Jodi didn't move. "What if I didn't get what I wanted?"

Miranda stared at her in confusion. "What do you mean?"

"What if I want this?" Jodi cupped her hands around Miranda's face and kissed her gently, then more deeply as their bodies melted against each other. Miranda wrapped her arms tightly around Jodi's slender frame, driving away the space between them. Her heart danced in her chest as they kissed, mouths open, tongues brushing against each other.

"Wait," Miranda's voice was hoarse, gently holding Jodi away from her. "I thought—"

"No more thinking," Jodi cut her off, pulling Miranda's hips firmly towards her as she kissed her again. Miranda's knees felt weak as desire spun through her like candy floss.

"Miranda, do you still want this?" Jodi asked, when they finally broke apart. Her voice was low and serious. "Because I really do. I've been stupidly focused on myself, on my tennis." She shook her head ruefully. "I couldn't see what was important to me."

"Tennis is important to you."

"Yes it is, and I hope it will continue to be for a long time to come. But so is living my life, and I think I can do both. I want this. I want you. I want to know you inside out, to learn all about you." Jodi ran her thumb across Miranda's jaw line. "I want to know what makes you tick. I want to discover what it's like to wake up with you lots of mornings in a row. Please tell me you want that too?"

Miranda looked searchingly into Jodi's eyes. "I do," she whispered.

"Then say we can be together because my heart is going to crumple up and die if you're not in love with me too."

Miranda broke into a grin, her eyes twinkling as she hitched her thumbs through Jodi's belt loops and tugged her towards her. "You're in love me?"

Jodi grinned back, winding her arms around Miranda's neck. "I might be."

"It sure sounds like you are."

"Hmm, maybe I am. I'm not sure," Jodi smirked, leaning back out of Miranda's reach.

"Really? What do you think you need to make up your mind?"

"Maybe some more of these," Jodi said, and pressed her lips slowly against Miranda's. Miranda kissed her back deeply, running her fingertips lightly up and down Jodi's back, cupping her hands around her backside as she pulled her in close.

"Is that making things any clearer?"

"Oh yes, quite a bit," Jodi's voice was husky, her lips moved away from Miranda's to trail kisses up and down her neck. "Do you think you could possibly love me?" Jodi murmured, her voice silken in Miranda's ear.

Miranda shivered, feeling the world open up around her. "Yes, I think that's quite possible."

"And what would I need to do to seal the deal?"

"I think," Miranda replied between kisses, "it's already done."

CHAPTER EIGHTEEN

"Miranda? Where are you?" Enid's voice floated through the hallway and up the stairs.

Miranda scrunched up her face, cracking open an eye to peek at the alarm clock next to her bed. 10:30am.

"I saw your car in the driveway," Enid called, "and your bag is on the hook, so I know you're in here. I'm coming up. It's too nice a day to sleep through."

Miranda registered the purposeful thud of Enid's shoes on the stairs, instantly regretting for the hundredth time giving her friend the spare key to her house.

"We'll get you up," Enid continued, thumping up the stairs, "and drown your sorrows in a cappuccino and a chocolate croissant down at the markets. The coffee is so strong there you'll forget all about your broken heart in the caffeine rush. Now wake up!" Enid threw open her door.

Miranda slowly opened her eyes and took in the shocked face of her best friend, standing stock still in the doorway.

"'Morning, Enid," she said.

Jodi shifted in her arms, snuggling in closer as she murmured, "Well, this isn't exactly how I'd planned our first morning together, darling."

"What the—" Enid spluttered, gripping the door frame dramatically. "Holy crap! I'm so sorry. I had no idea. I wouldn't have let myself in but I never in a million years expected—"

"It's okay," Miranda laughed, pulling the sheet up a little higher around them. "Surprise," she grinned sheepishly.

"Surprise indeed!" Enid hovered in the doorway for a moment before bounding over to the bed. She perched on the end of it and tucked her feet up.

"This is huge news! Now tell me all about it," Enid demanded. "How did this happen?"

"Enid!" Miranda protested.

"Good morning, Enid," Jodi said sweetly. "And how is Abby this morning?"

"Abby!" Enid cried, jumping off the bed. "She's waiting for us in the car. I'll go and get her."

"No, wait Enid," said Miranda. She suppressed a laugh. "Why don't you guys go for the cappuccinos and the croissants and bring us back some when you're done? If that's alright with you, Jodi?"

"Sounds perfect."

Enid looked torn. "Are you sure? We could wait for you guys to get up."

"I think Jodi and I will just take it slowly this morning."

"Of course, of course." Enid nodded knowingly. "See you in a couple of hours then."

Enid banged the door closed behind her, clattering back down the stairs.

"Huge news!" she cried jubilantly again up the stairs, letting herself out Miranda's front door.

"Good morning," Miranda turned to Jodi, gazing into her eyes with a smile as she tenderly ran her thumb over Jodi's bruised lips.

"Good morning, yourself." Jodi kissed her lightly, trailing her fingertips over Miranda's chest. The dappled morning light bathed the bedroom in soft yellows. A light summer breeze was playing with the curtains. Miranda groaned, giving herself over to their kisses. Her skin felt different. She felt silken and lithe between the sheets as their bodies found each other again.

"We might need to ring Enid," Jodi whispered, her breath catching as Miranda lightly kissed the sensitive skin down her neck.

"Why is that?" Miranda paused, suddenly confused.

"I think we're going to need more than just chocolate croissants this morning."

* * *

Jodi stood in the tunnel waiting for the signal to enter the court. Her opponent stood in front of her, nervously tapping her racket bag. They didn't look at each other, each trying to retain her inner focus and concentration. She was distantly aware of the crowd, buzzing with conversation and expectation as they waited for the umpire's announcement.

"Ladies and Gentlemen," the umpire began. "Match One on court three today is Richards versus Sariovski. Please, welcome the players."

Jodi strode out of the tunnel purposefully; she set her bags down on her designated bench and got her rackets out. The crowd was larger than she had expected. She busied herself tightening her shoelaces. Jason had warned her that even the opening matches and the relatively unknown players still drew sizeable crowds at the US Open and he hadn't been wrong. She repositioned her cap and stood up, loosening her limbs with a little on-the-spot jog.

"Please come to the net for the toss," the umpire called.

Jodi made her way to the net and won the toss for service. In the stands, her eyes found Miranda, and her heart swelled. Miranda gave her a thumbs up; next to her in the coach's box, Jason did the same. She was so glad Miranda had flown to New York in time for the first match. It felt right to see her up there next to Jase.

Jodi moved to the baseline. She accepted a volley of balls from the ball boy and tucked them into her skirt, giving one an experimental bounce. She took a deep breath and signaled to her opponent that she was ready to start their warm up. No matter what happened here, no matter how tough her opponents, how grueling the matches, or how unrelenting the sun, the bad line calls, or the merciless heat, Jodi was ready.

And now that she and Miranda had found each other, she had already won.

Bella Books, Inc.

Women. Books. Even Better Together.

P.O. Box 10543
Tallahassee, FL 32302

Phone: 800-729-4992
www.bellabooks.com